MW00946338

Boundless

The Queen's Alpha Series, Volume 6

W.J. May

Published by Dark Shadow Publishing, 2018.

This is a work of fiction. Similarities to real people, places, or events are entirely coincidental.

BOUNDLESS

First edition. May 2, 2018.

Written by W.J. May.

Also by W.J. May

Bit-Lit Series
Lost Vampire
Cost of Blood
Price of Death

Blood Red Series
Courage Runs Red
The Night Watch
Marked by Courage
Forever Night

Daughters of Darkness: Victoria's Journey
Victoria
Huntress
Coveted (A Vampire & Paranormal Romance)
Twisted
Daughter of Darkness - Victoria - Box Set

Hidden Secrets Saga
Seventh Mark - Part 1
Seventh Mark - Part 2
Marked By Destiny
Compelled
Fate's Intervention
Chosen Three
The Hidden Secrets Saga: The Complete Series

Kerrigan Chronicles
Stopping Time
A Passage of Time

Mending Magic Series
Lost Souls

Paranormal Huntress Series
Never Look Back
Coven Master
Alpha's Permission
Blood Bonding
Oracle of Nightmares
Shadows in the Night

Evermore
Forever
Boundless
Prophecy
Protected

The Senseless Series
Radium Halos
Radium Halos - Part 2
Nonsense

Standalone
Shadow of Doubt (Part 1 & 2)
Five Shades of Fantasy
Shadow of Doubt - Part 1
Shadow of Doubt - Part 2
Four and a Half Shades of Fantasy
Dream Fighter
What Creeps in the Night
Forest of the Forbidden
Arcane Forest: A Fantasy Anthology
The First Fantasy Box Set

Watch for more at https://www.facebook.com/USA-TODAY-Bestseller-WJ-May-Author-141170442608149/.

THE QUEEN'S ALPHA SERIES

BOUNDLESS

USA TODAY BESTSELLING AUTHOR
W . J .   M A Y

THIS E-BOOK IS LICENSED for your personal enjoyment only. This e-book may not be re-sold or given away to other people. If you would like to share this book with another person, please purchase an additional copy for each recipient. If you're reading this book and did not purchase it, or it was not purchased for your use only, then please return to Smashwords.com and purchase your own copy. Thank you for respecting the hard work of the author.

Have You Read the C.o.K Series?

The Chronicles of Kerrigan
Book I - *Rae of Hope* is FREE!

BOOK TRAILER:

http://www.youtube.com/watch?v=gILAwXxx8MU

How hard do you have to shake the family tree to find the truth about the past?

Fifteen-year-old Rae Kerrigan never really knew her family's history. Her mother and father died when she was young and it is only when she accepts a scholarship to the prestigious Guilder Boarding School in England that a mysterious family secret is revealed.

Will the sins of the father be the sins of the daughter?

As Rae struggles with new friends, a new school and a star-struck forbidden love, she must also face the ultimate challenge: receive a tattoo on her sixteenth birthday with specific powers that may bind her to an unspeakable darkness. It's up to Rae to undo the dark evil in her family's past and have a ray of hope for her future.

Find W.J. May

Website:
http://www.wanitamay.yolasite.com
Facebook:
https://www.facebook.com/pages/Author-WJ-May-FAN-PAGE/141170442608149
Newsletter:
SIGN UP FOR W.J. May's Newsletter to find out about new releases, updates, cover reveals and even freebies!
http://eepurl.com/97aYf

Boundless Blurb:

SHE WILL FIGHT FOR what is hers.

Magic runs thicker than blood...

As the final battle approaches, the exiled princess finally returns home... only to find that things are not as they seem.

After a shocking discovery leaves them scrambling, Katerina and her friends find themselves faced with the toughest problem yet—finding an enemy they can kill. Alliances are tested, traitors are revealed, and bonds are stretched to the brink as the two armies march towards each other.

Can Katerina find a way to save the one person she thought was already lost? Can she unlock the secrets of her family's ancient power in time? Or will she find herself losing more than just a crown and a kingdom?

Only time will tell.

Be careful who you trust. Even the devil was once an angel.

The Queen's Alpha Series

Eternal
Everlasting
Unceasing
Evermore
Forever
Boundless
Prophecy
Protected
Foretelling
Revelation
Betrayal

BOUNDLESS 9

Resolved

Chapter 1

"CASSIEL—NO!"

Serafina flew to the bars of her cell as her brother flew the opposite direction. Before anyone could stop him he'd grabbed the prince by the throat, lifting him high in the air then smashing him against the stone wall with terrifying force. The others heard a chilling crack, mixed with his sister's screams, and saw a stream of blood trickle down into the dirt.

There was a good chance the prince was dead already. And the fae clearly didn't care.

"It wasn't his fault," the lovely fae gasped again, half-collapsing where she stood. "Please, listen to me!"

But there was no getting through to her brother. Not now. Not about this.

His entire face had transformed with the purest sort of rage. It had hardened every line. Sharpened every angle. Blazed like liquid fire in his dark eyes. His hand tightened, and a broken gasp escaped from the prince's throat, a gasp so soft Katerina could barely hear it.

Her eyes flew automatically to Dylan, but the ranger was lost in his own world.

He'd hardly noticed the violence going on behind him. The fact that the crown prince of the High Kingdom was about to die. He was standing exactly where the others had left him, staring through the bars of the cell like he was lost in a dream.

"I saw them drag you away..." he said faintly, gazing at the weeping prisoner in a sort of daze. "There was blood, strips of your clothes... nothing was left."

Serafina saw her chance and took it, turning from one man to the other. "They dragged me back here," she sobbed. "Threw me in the dungeon. They would have done a lot more than that, but Kailas stopped them. Please, Dylan—this isn't what you think!"

Katerina's lips fell open as she took a step back. She couldn't help but notice the tender way the lovely girl said her brother's name. It was the same way Katerina said Dylan. Like a caress.

"Cass—*please*!" She threw herself at the bars of her cell again, shaking with uncontrollable tears. "Dylan, do something! Make him stop!"

It was too much. *Way* too much.

Katerina took another step back. Then another. Her head was spinning. The floor was tilting wildly underfoot. No matter how many times she looked at the scene in front of her, she couldn't get it to make sense. What was her brother doing down here? Why wasn't he fighting back? How was it possible that, after all these years, the princess of the fae was still somehow alive?

Alive *and* screaming.

"We need to shut her up," Rose muttered frantically to no one in particular. "They're going to come and investigate. They're going to find us..."

But Serafina was in a place beyond consolation. Her wide, dark eyes were fixed on the pair of men on the other side of the chamber. Her knuckles were white as they gripped the bars of her iron cage.

"Brother," she cried, slipping back to older times when siblings called each other as such, instead of using formal names, "listen to me! It wasn't him. He was under a spell!"

A spell?

It was at that moment that Katerina noticed several things at once.

Her brother was still tall—yes. But he was also somehow broken. There was a delicacy to the way he was holding himself as his legs dangled helplessly in the air.

Her brother was still handsome—it was true. But there were shadows on his radiant face. A sort of dullness beneath the dirt and matted blood, as if he hadn't seen the sun in a long time.

But the last thing she noticed was perhaps the most telling. The most telling, and yet the most utterly confusing all at the same time.

Her brother hadn't been standing against the wall when they'd come in. He'd been chained.

"Cassiel..." Katerina said tentatively.

At the sound of her voice, Dylan snapped out of his trance. He glanced over his shoulder at her stricken face before turning to where his best friend in the world was slowly and methodically killing her brother. A savage kind of hate twisted the fae's lovely features as he choked the life out of the prince's body. Reveling in every tremor that shook through him. Every broken gasp.

It was all-consuming. Devouring him from the inside out. He was legitimately unaware of the world around him and jumped slightly when Dylan put a steadying hand on his arm.

"He's chained," the ranger said softly, eyes sweeping the rusted iron manacle that encircled the prince's neck. "Listen to your sister. She's asking you to stop."

A muscle flexed in the back of the fae's jaw as his eyes found the chain for the first time, but one way or another he seemed physically incapable of pulling himself back. That dark fire was still glowing in his eyes, and for a moment Katerina was reminded of the time when Cassiel himself was trapped under a spell—deep in the heart of Laurelwood. She'd never been afraid of him until that day, never understood the true devastation of which he was capable. She understood it now.

"This man..." he hissed, grinding the prince deeper into the wall, "this man is responsible for every bit of pain you and I have ever known. He set our world on fire, just so he could laugh as he watched it burn. I'm going to kill him, Dylan. And you're going to let me. I'm going to kill him for us and for Katerina. She can't do it on her own."

His grip tightened even more, but at the sound of her name the prince showed the first signs of life. One battered hand came up to Cassiel's wrist as his feet twitched reflexively against the wall.

"...Katerina?" It was like hearing a ghost. His voice was no more than a lifeless whisper as his eyes searched desperately in the dark. "Katy?"

The princess' heart lurched. Hearing the childhood nickname that had been special between just them. Hearing how weak her brother sounded when he said it. How close to the end.

A thousand images flashed through her mind. A thousand images she'd worked so hard over the last few months to forget. Images of Kailas and her playing together out in the woods—building tree forts and making castles out of clay. Of the books they'd shared, and the games they'd played, and the countless hours they'd sat trapped under the churlish gaze of the same droning tutor. Of the time their father had taken the five-year-old prince hunting for the first time and he'd shot a young deer. He'd grinned proudly in front of their father but had been so traumatized that he'd crept into Katerina's chambers that night and cried himself to sleep. He'd slept there every day for a week.

Images of a bright-eyed, playful little boy, turning into a tall, capable adolescent. Someone a little more serious. Someone a little less charming. Eventually that charm vanished entirely, leaving a cold, cruel young man in its wake. A young man who wouldn't think twice before delivering his own brand of justice. A young man who secretly frightened his twin sister, though she'd never say.

It was something she'd grown accustomed to over the years. A silent heartbreak, the weight of which she'd grown so used to she scarcely felt it anymore. All that changed the night he killed their father. The night he tried to have her killed as well. When he'd stood at the gate of the castle and sent his monstrous hounds running after her in the woods, something between them had died.

But *this* man. Tired, trembling, unwilling to fight... she didn't recognize him at all.

Cautious and pale, she stepped out of the shadows into the faint light of the candles scattered in the cell. His eyes found her, and for a moment brother and sister went completely still.

How can things be so different, yet feel exactly the same?

Everything about him was familiar. From his dark eyes, to the proud curve of his brow, to the softer lines of his mouth. He had their father's powerful presence, but their mother's sweet smile. It was a beautiful combination. One Katerina had been jealous of many times.

His clothes were familiar, too, the same finery they both used to wear around the castle. Only, now they were stained with a mixture of dirt and blood. His hair was matted with it as well, longer than Katerina had ever seen it—hanging just beneath his chin—and deep shadows had hollowed out the space beneath his eyes, as if he hadn't slept in a long while.

He was dying, still helplessly choking in Cassiel's hands, but even so his lips curved up into a tortured smile. "...you changed your hair."

For whatever reason, that was the breaking point.

"Let him go," Katerina said urgently, striding across the chamber and gripping Cassiel's arm. "Cass, you need to let go."

"Please let go," Serafina echoed. She had slid down to the floor of her cell, her legs unable to support her for a second longer. "*Please.*"

"Listen to your sister," Dylan pressed, one hand easing gently along the fae's wrist as he attempted to loosen that impossible grip. "Just for a moment, just for now... let go."

Cassiel pulled in a sharp breath as the conflict raged behind his eyes. After everything he'd been through, after all these years, what they were asking him to do was almost impossible.

But it was his sister who was asking. His resurrected sister, back from the dead.

A single spark of light penetrated the darkness as he stared into Kailas' eyes. Then, in a single motion, he released the prince and stepped back, turning to his sister instead. He didn't see the way the prince fell forward, held up only by his chains. He no longer cared. Other, more pressing, matters now occupied his mind.

"I have to get you out of here," he murmured, one hand cupping the side of his sister's face as the other ran experimentally up the bars. "If we can get enough leverage on the base—"

"Here," Tanya said gently, coming up behind him. "Let me."

The air around them shimmered as she suddenly sprouted into a man about five times her usual size—a man who looked vaguely patterned off one of the cave trolls they'd met back in the camp at Pora. Serafina shrank back in terror, but Cassiel never let go of her hand as his girlfriend gripped the bars at the base and ripped them swiftly from the stone. A second later she was her old self again, lifting the rusted iron with a coaxing smile to allow the frightened girl to crawl out.

She did so slowly. Cautiously. Like at any moment they might snap back shut.

Who did this to you? Katerina wondered as she stared with wide, dilated eyes. Those same eyes drifted back to her brother in the dark. *Who did this to you both?*

The second she was free, brother and sister grabbed each other in a fierce embrace. Cassiel buried his face in her neck, gripping her like the world was about to end as she collapsed with an exhausted sigh into his arms. They stood there for what felt like a small eternity, oblivious to the passage of time, whispering to each other in their native tongue, then Serafina tentatively pulled away. Her eyes swept across the length of the chamber for a moment, coming to rest upon the battered prince, before she sprang across the room and did the last thing anyone would expect.

She kissed him.

Katerina's jaw fell wide open as Cassiel stared at his sister in shock. Dylan, who was still having trouble stringing together full sentences, gaped in disbelief until the two finally pulled apart.

A warm smile was stirring in her eyes. One that was reflected by Kailas.

"I've wanted to do that for a very long time."

Broken as he was, the prince managed a soft laugh, straining gently towards her in his chains. "I told you we would," he said quietly, staring at her with adoration, completely oblivious to the rest of the people staring on in shock. "You didn't believe me."

She laughed as well, a bright, tinkling sound that seemed to light up the room. "Well, you have to admit," she glanced back at the cell, "our chances didn't look good..."

It might have been a touching moment, but to everyone else it fell short.

Cassiel's eyes had snapped shut the second he heard his little sister laugh. The rest of them had started glancing nervously towards the stairs, convinced they were about to be discovered, and Katerina couldn't seem to wrench her eyes away from her brother.

They had come here with a specific plan. A clear purpose that was supposed to put an end to this mess once and for all. To get the five kingdoms back on the straight and narrow. But all that was muddied now. Confused to the point where Katerina didn't know what should happen next.

"Kat." She started as a voice spoke softly in her ear. It was Aidan. One of the only people in the room who seemed to have kept his head throughout the entire debacle. "We can't stay here. The girl was screaming. The guards will be coming soon to see what's happened."

Never let it be said that vampires aren't level-headed...

The princess nodded faintly and tried to summon her wits. Coming to the castle had been her idea. Kailas—for better or worse—was her responsibility. Whatever their next move was going to be, it would be up to her as well.

"Serafina."

It was the first time the two had spoken directly, and the breathtaking fae looked back in surprise. Their eyes met for a split second before Katerina forced herself to continue.

"You said Kailas was under a spell. What kind of spell? Whose spell was it?"

Even as she said the words, there wasn't a doubt in her mind as to the answer. They had been chased all over the five kingdoms by a dark wizard tormenting their every step, and now she was to understand that her twin brother had fallen prey to the same evil magic?

The two were one and the same. Part of the same elaborate plot. She was sure of it. But, certain as she was, the princess never could have predicted what would happen next.

"It was mine."

Katerina recognized the voice before she even turned around. Felt it stab her chest like a blade before ripping out the other side. Leaving her in a thousand shattered pieces.

Alwyn.

The second she turned around, there he was. Standing in the frame of the doorway. Looking exactly as she remembered in swirling robes. His eyes lit and sparkling. His wrinkled face framed by a sea of billowing ivory hair. The only thing different was the knife he was holding in one hand. A knife that was pointing directly at her brother's heart.

"Well, well, well..." His eyes glittered as he stepped out of the shadows and into the light. "...look who's all grown up."

Chapter 2

"I CAN'T SAY IT'S GOOD to see you, Katerina. But it's certainly been a long time."

The entire room froze in an instant. There wasn't a sound, there wasn't a breath. Ten people stood perfectly still. A host of ghostly statues, waiting to get tapped back into action. Their muscles tensed and coiled, their bodies ready for the command.

But it was a command that would never come.

No matter how long she stood there, no matter how long she stared into her mentor's eyes—her oldest friend—the princess couldn't reconcile what she was seeing.

"Well, say something, darling," he murmured. "Don't leave us in suspense." He took a step forward, and all at once the deafening silence shattered into a million pieces.

"LEAVE HER ALONE!"

Much to everyone's surprise, the command came from Kailas. The second the wizard took a step towards the princess, he threw himself against his chains, fighting to get in between his sister and Alwyn.

Triggered, the room came alive once more. Except, no one seemed to know what to do.

Tanya stepped towards Katerina then froze, while Rose melted back against the wall. Aidan's fangs came down with a faint hiss, while Cassiel's eyes darted protectively to his sister. Torn between two enemies Dylan didn't know where to look, but his fingers wrapped around his blade.

Alwyn saw the covert movement and smiled, waving his own knife like a chiding finger. "Lift a hand, ranger, and this dagger will fly straight into the prince's heart. It's bewitched to do so and will slice through anything in its way."

Dylan looked as though that wasn't exactly a deal-breaker, but Serafina threw herself in front of Kailas with a silent gasp. Arms stretched out like a shield. An untamed fire blazing in her eyes.

"Sweetheart, please..."

The prince spoke softly, but Katerina still heard loud and clear. Each word resonating like a drum. Sweetheart? She didn't think her brother was capable of such a word.

"Sera..." Kailas tried to get her to move, but his wrists were chained—up and out to the side, keeping him standing, like he was lashed to a cross. "You heard what he said, it won't help."

The girl completely ignored him. Staying right where she was. Staring out with that same deadly determination at the blade. If it pierced his heart, it would have to go through hers to do so.

"How sweet," Alwyn chuckled, lowering the blade though it stayed ready in his hand. "The world's most tragic love story." His eyes swept briskly over the others, cold and mocking, two expressions Katerina had never seen on his face. "I'm afraid the rest of you are a little late to this party. Day in, and day out. So close, yet so far. Never quite able to *touch*..."

The couple flinched back, like his words carried an actual sting, and he laughed again.

"Unlike you!" With a broad smile, he turned to Katerina. "It looks as though your own romance has blossomed quite happily. Present circumstances excluded..."

"I said leave her alone!" Kailas shouted, straining desperately against the rusted iron that imprisoned him, trying to get to his sister. "You will not SPEAK to her—"

Alwyn's smile grew cold and his voice slithered out like a snake. *"Sleep."*

A strange look passed over the prince's face. As if he'd been plunged into shadow. His pupils dilated, and his muscles jerked reflexively. But before he could say a word, his eyes fluttered shut and he slumped forward, strands of matted hair spilling into his lifeless face.

"Kailas!" Katerina exclaimed, surprised by her own concern. She took an automatic step towards him then caught herself, turning to her mentor instead. "I don't understand... the dark wizard. The one we asked you to find... you were never looking for him. All this time. It was you?" She stared at him. "It was you."

Alwyn cocked his head appraisingly, the way he used to do when she asked an especially astute question back in school. "It sounds to me like you understand perfectly."

Even now, even with him admitting it, the princess couldn't come to terms. She kept waiting for the other shoe to drop. For the wizard to call her 'dear one.' For him to admit he'd been making the world's worst joke and help them cut Kailas down.

Kailas.

Her eyes flashed back to her brother, hanging limp in his chains, before turning back, eyes wide with dawning horror. "...you put him under a spell?"

The wizard nodded, flipping the blade back and forth with surprisingly practiced hands. "Yes, but not recently. You remember your brother's hounds?" His eyes narrowed with a twisted smile. "Of course, you do. Well, there's a reason hell hounds are banned within the borders of the five kingdoms. Anything that hails from the badlands is spawned in pestilence and shadow."

Katerina remembered the day the puppies had arrived at the castle. A gift for the young prince. A package with no sender. A present with no note.

"When I got them for Kailas, he was only ten years old. They've had the last eight years to work their darkness into him. Twisting it slowly through his veins, like a venom. It took a long time, but I was patient. I had to be. I had everything to gain, and nothing to lose."

"*Malacos*," Serafina spat out in her native tongue. "You are a monster."

Katerina jumped in her skin, remembering the woodland princess for the first time. "And her?" She gestured blindly, unable to tear her eyes away. "All these years—"

"Yes," Alwyn interrupted, "she's been here. It wasn't that difficult to do. To the guards, she was just another prisoner, and your father never came down here himself. Your brother found out, of course. When my power was strong over him, he never said a word. By the time he started to break free, well..." He glanced at the chains and shrugged. "Other accommodations had to be made."

Katerina jerked back like she'd been slapped in the face, making the dreadful connection for the first time. A strange chill seeped up through her legs as the stale dampness that hung in the air worked its way into her very bones. Leaving her flushed and shivering at the same time. "You've been—" Her voice cracked, and she had to start again. "You've been keeping him down here? For how long?"

She remembered what the servant had said about no one having seen the prince in a long time. She remembered the state of his room. Pristine. Abandoned.

Alwyn didn't answer. He merely smiled.

A surge of anger welled up in the princess' chest—thawing the frozen grip that had taken hold. Her blood felt like it was near boiling, drowning out all her other senses, and when she took a compulsive step forward Dylan's hand shot out like lightning to hold her back.

The wizard took in every detail with keen interest.

"How is that even possible?" she demanded. "The council, the guards! People have to wonder why they haven't seen his face!"

"Oh, he goes out sometimes." Alwyn wiggled his fingers in the air and black smoke seemed to ooze out of them. Drifting past Serafina's shining eyes and fluttering around the prince's face. "I have to admit, he's been getting more and more difficult to control. I blame this one."

His eyes came to rest on Serafina, still standing like a sentry between them.

Kat's gaze shifted side to side, trying to look from her beloved mentor, to her brother, to Cass' sister.

"Children of the stars," Alwyn murmured, almost to himself. "They're gifted with their own magic, you know. Far different than my sorcery." He flashed a quick smile at Cassiel, who was rigid as a stone. "In this case, your little sister was the perfect antidote to my poison. She kept him grounded. Kept him sane. I probably should have just killed her outright, but she's been useful in other ways. As leverage. As the only thing in the world our beloved prince couldn't bear to see destroyed... until now." His eyes lit up with a dangerous smile. "Now his dear twin sister is home."

Katerina shook her head, eyes shining with tears that refused to fall. All these years, all this time... it was right under her very nose. Her brother was being slowly poisoned, and she never even saw it.

She thought he'd simply changed. Turned her back on him, when he needed her the most.

"But you were happy!" she insisted. "You raised us, you were part of the family! I've known you all my life, and you were happy—"

"I was a *prisoner*!" Alwyn spat. "One of the last remaining wizards, when the rest of my kind was hunted to the brink of extinction. Forced to work as a bodyguard, a nanny. Bound by magic, so I was unable to leave the castle walls." He met the baffled look on Katerina's face with a mirthless laugh. "Why do you think I never came with you on any of the royal outings? Why do you think I always stayed behind?" His eyes burned and the wisps of smoke still hovering around Kailas' face seemed to crawl inside his skin. "This castle has been my prison. But now, it will be my greatest triumph. When I strike down the last of the Damaris bloodline and burn it all to the ground."

Fire and brimstone. Death and destruction. The total annihilation of her line.

Yet, the princess could think of only a single question...

"How did you know about Dylan?"

There was a blurred movement somewhere behind her as Alwyn looked up in surprise. The bewitched knife stopped spinning, freezing in mid-air.

"How did I—"

"You said that my own romance has blossomed," Katerina said sharply, quoting his exact words. "But you've only seen us together a few minutes, and we've had next to no interaction in that time. So, I'll ask again... How could you possibly know that?"

It was a clear point for the princess, but the wizard still had tricks up his sleeve. He rocked back on his heels, eyes sparkling, looking almost proud. "Well spotted, Katy."

"Don't call me that," she hissed, stepping instinctively closer to her brother. "Only *he* calls me that. It isn't yours to use."

"You asked how I knew about your relationship when, in fact, it goes much deeper than that," Alwyn replied with a smile. "In truth, there is very little I don't know about what you've been doing since striking out on your own."

He and the princess stared at each other for a long moment. Then something clicked.

"The old woman we met by Redfern Peak," she said slowly. "The one who claimed to be a witch and gave me that seeing stone... that was you."

The wizard's eyes twinkled, and she knew she was right. She remembered the way the woman had looked curiously over her companions before giving Katerina the stone—a way to contact Alwyn directly and tell him all about her plans. When she'd looked back to thank her, just seconds later, the woman was already gone. Vanished into thin air. Only a pitch-black raven remained. A raven the princess was just starting to realize had popped up along several points of their journey.

"But I thought you couldn't leave the castle," she objected. "You said it yourself—you were bound by magic to stay here."

"My corporeal form, yes," Alwyn conceded. "But there are other, less convenient ways to travel. At any rate, it was incredibly difficult to maintain. I quickly realized I was going to have to find a more permanent means of keeping track of you."

Katerina hesitated with a sudden sense of dread. "A more permanent means—"

"Yes," Alwyn interjected, "and it was a great success. I've been kept very well informed of your every activity. Well," his voice suddenly sharpened, "until recently..."

"I don't understand." Katerina shook her head. "What does that mean?"

Alwyn cocked his head with a little smile. "Isn't it obvious, my dear?" He spread his arms wide, gesturing to her friends. "There is a spy in your midst."

THERE'S A SPY IN OUR *midst?*

When your entire life revolves around a tight-knit group of people, people who have sworn their loyalty to you, people who hold your life in their hands... there's no coming back from that.

Be careful who you trust; even the devil was once an angel.

The words seemed to stab Katerina in the heart, as if Alwyn's knife had pierced her. She sucked her breath in sharply as she stared at Alwyn for a split second, then dropped her eyes to the floor. Not because she thought he was lying, but because she didn't see any way that he could *not* be telling the truth.

And how could she not have known?

There were too many coincidences. Too many close calls. Times when royal guards had shown up out of nowhere, even when they'd been so careful to cover their tracks. The fact that they were expected in Belaria. How the tide of the river had shifted, forcing them into the hands of the Carpathian queen. Times when their 'bad luck' seemed almost too much to take.

Only now, Katerina knew it wasn't 'bad luck' at all. It was Alwyn. Even a hundred miles away from the castle, the man was still holding the strings. Steering her in the direction he wanted. Deftly manipulating her course. Depending upon the information relayed to him by his trusted spy.

But who?

Her eyes flickered around the room, resting on each one in turn, before coming to a sudden stop. That feeling of dread that had gnawed away at her since they entered the castle froze over like a weighted stone. Dropping her stomach to the floor. Making her blood run cold.

Stay away from vampires, princess. We're monsters, haven't you heard?

She remembered the way he'd materialized out of thin air that night he'd saved her in the tavern stock room. Putting him in exactly the right place. At exactly the right time. The way he'd stayed with them from place to place—well beyond the parameters of his mission, even after they decided not to go to Rorque. The way he'd been assigned to be their guide.

'*How did a vampire become the sole representative of the rebel camps?*' she'd asked him.

She remembered his quiet laugh. The way those mesmerizing eyes of his had lured her in.

'*Oh, you know...I ate all the other contenders.*'

Aidan was staring at Alwyn. Everyone else was staring at him. It took him a second to realize what was going on. His lips parted, and he took an actual step backwards in surprise.

"You can't be serious," he breathed, those luminous eyes resting on each one of them in turn. "After everything we've been through, after all this time... you think it's me."

Five pairs of probing eyes stared back at him. The friends said not a word.

He glanced swiftly at Alwyn before turning back to his former companions. A look of true anger flashed in his eyes. Making him look cold, frightening, predatory. Like a real vampire. It was hard to remember that's what he was. Somehow, he always seemed to make them forget.

"You think it's me." It wasn't a question. This time, his eyes were fixed directly on Katerina.

They lure you in. Tell gentle lies. Make you feel safe.

She'd been absolutely entranced by him that night in the forest. Dazzled by his unearthly beauty. Captivated by those hypnotic eyes. She'd let down her walls and let him come closer. She'd fallen asleep in his arms...

The very essence of their nature demands the extinction of ours.

He was never scared before a fight. Never hesitated before jumping into battle. Almost as if he already knew the outcome. The only man not affected by the siren's call.

Some say they don't even have a soul...

Katerina met his eyes for a suspended moment. Then she turned back to the wizard.

"Just go, vampire. There's no place for you here."

She hardly recognized her own voice. It was so callous, so cold. She hardly recognized the words she was saying—couldn't believe she was saying them to Aidan.

Neither could he.

He stayed right where he was, staring at her in open shock. The light of the candles flickered desperately in his dark eyes, like the last vestiges of a dying hope. But still, he couldn't bring himself to move. He clung to that hope with everything he had. With every bit of that impossible strength.

His eyes flashed again, and he was about to say something, when a sinister chuckle echoed through the air. He turned instead to Alwyn, frozen with that same blank stare.

"An alliance is a far cry from friendship, vampire. And, despite best wishes, friendship is not an option for your kind. It seems the Damaris princess is no exception to that line of thought."

The words unfroze him. Unlocked his rigid stance. One second, he was standing there. The next, he was sweeping briskly out of the dungeon without a backwards glance. It wasn't until he got to the stairs that he came to a sudden pause, like some invisible force was holding him back. His shoulders tensed, and he cast a parting glance over his shoulder, finding the princess once more.

"Good luck," he murmured softly, eyes flashing to the wizard. "You're going to need it."

Then he was gone.

For a moment, all was quiet. Kailas was still unconscious, Serafina was concerned with little else than his well-being, and the five friends were shaken to the core. Katerina could have lived and died in that moment. Replaying every moment. Every micro-expression. Hearing every stricken word echo in her mind.

Then Alwyn threw back his head with a roaring laugh.

It shook the stillness. As jarring as it was cruel. Dylan's hand tightened upon the princess' arm, and it was taking everything bit of resolve he had not to throw his blade.

"Well, *that* was certainly entertaining! Wasn't it, dear one?"

Dear one.

How Katerina had longed to hear him say the words before, resurrecting the pet name he'd called her since she was just a child. How she'd longed to hear him recant, to say he'd made the whole thing up, to come back to her side. Now, she couldn't imagine him there in the first place.

She gritted her teeth, and her eyes danced with crimson flames. "Don't call me that—"

She started speaking, then cut herself short. It was only then she realized something incredibly important. Just a minor detail, but one that changed absolutely everything.

Alwyn hadn't been speaking to her. He'd been speaking to Rose.

The princess whirled around in shock as the beautiful shifter cringed farther into the stone wall. She hadn't said a word since Alwyn had entered the dungeon. All that she'd said before had been warnings, begging the others to postpone their mission. To turn around. To flee.

"*You.*" Kat felt the venom rise in the back of her throat.

Rose didn't deny it. Nor did she freeze, the way Aidan had. The second she and Katerina locked eyes, she bowed her head. The game was finished. Her long charade had come to an end.

"Yes, *her.*" Alwyn was still laughing quietly, wiping his eyes as yet another horrific piece of the puzzle fell into place. "*Not* the vampire you so unceremoniously sent on his way. Poor thing's self-esteem will probably never recover. That's if the castle guards haven't gotten him already."

A rip of terror swept through the princess and she almost called out for him right then, but a part of her knew it was no use. Some bridges, once burned, could never be repaired.

"But how did you do it?" She turned back to Rose in a sort of daze. "We were always on the move, never in the same place twice. How did you keep in contact with him?"

With trembling hands, the shifter reached into her coat and pulled out a small, blunted sapphire. A gem that looked remarkably similar to the tiny amethyst Katerina had lost.

"A seeing stone," Kat breathed. "You had your own?"

Rose didn't answer, but the stone slipped from her fingers as her eyes dropped back to the ground. She couldn't seem to stop shaking. She couldn't seem to stop the tears that were silently sliding down her face.

Bit by bit, Katerina started to piece things together. From the very beginning, Rose was formidable enough that she was one of the only people Dylan trusted to keep watch at night on her own. There would have been plenty of time for her to sneak away and use the stone discreetly. She had worked her way into the perfect position to hear every plan, every destination. To report on their every move, warning Alwyn ahead of time, influencing things still to come.

Katerina remembered when they left Belaria and the gang was arguing about how the guards had possibly been expecting them before Dylan's subsequent arrest. The ranger had sworn that no one was around for miles, that they'd left no tracks. '*It's impossible,*' he'd cursed. Not many people had heard the shifter's quiet response. '*Maybe you're not as good as you think you are...*'

The group of friends hadn't happened upon her at the Talsing Sanctuary. She'd been waiting for them. And from what Katerina suddenly remembered, she must have been waiting for a long time.

"You told me you'd gone to the sanctuary after your village was destroyed," the princess said in a quiet voice—seething, but still too surprised to do much more. "That your mother had sent you to find Michael, told you that he could help save your life."

There was a brief pause, then Rose finally lifted her head. Stared back at the princess with a truly heartbreaking expression. "That was all true. Only... something happened to me in between."

Alwyn. Alwyn happened to her in between.

"He told me your family was responsible for the death of mine. He told me there was a way I could avenge them. A way that I could help." Like flipping a switch the fearless, confident shifter dissolved in front of their very eyes. Leaving a scared, trembling girl in her wake. "He sent me ahead to the monastery, told me you'd be coming. That he was going to send you there. Told me to wait."

It was a genius plan. It made perfect sense.

But at the same time... it didn't.

"You didn't want to come here," Katerina said slowly, vaguely aware that she was stepping onto dangerous ground. "You tried to stop us from telling Alwyn, from sending the message."

"Message?" Alwyn straightened with sudden attention. "I never received any message."

Rose froze dead still, caught between the two groups. On the one hand, it looked like she was dying to return to Katerina and the others, to slip back into the fold. On the other, it looked as though she knew that time had passed. She'd burned the bridge with them, just as surely as the one with the wizard was crumbling before her very eyes.

Then Katerina's face lightened in amazement. "You shot it down."

She remembered sending out the last raven, then breaking up to pack. By the time she'd finished getting ready, Rose was just returning to the camp. Handing Cassiel his bow.

The wizard's face sharpened as his eyes swept over the shifter the way one might look at a disobedient pet. "Did you now..."

"You didn't want us to come here," Katerina continued incredulously. "You knew that he would find us. You kept trying to get us to turn back."

Rose's lips parted, but she was at a loss for words. A kind of helplessness had settled over her. An expression that somehow reminded Katerina vaguely of her brother.

"But the berries," she blurted, remembering her late-night hallucinogenic experience in the woods. An excursion that almost ended in her jumping off a cliff. "You knew exactly what those berries were. You tried to kill me—"

"I wasn't supposed to do that," Rose whispered. The tears continued to fall, but her words had broken free—pouring out of her in a rush. "Up until then, even Alwyn was trying to protect you. I just thought...I thought that if you were gone, it would all be over. The plan would be ruined, the wizard would forget about me, and I could just slip away." Her eyes grew distant as they gazed into the future, a future she would never have. "I could stay with the others and go to the rebel camps myself. I could fight in the resistance. Find another pack maybe..."

"Alwyn was trying to *protect* her?" It was the first time Dylan had spoken, and the words hissed angrily through the air. "An avalanche, a rockslide, hundreds of royal soldiers hounding our every step. Arrested in Belaria. Captured again in Carpathia... and you say he was *protecting* her?"

At a glance, everything he said made perfect sense. It was a miracle that, after everything they'd been through, the princess had survived. But the longer she thought about it, stringing those events into a precarious timeline, the more Katerina realized it wasn't exactly true.

The rockslide had merely stopped them from going to the safe house. The avalanche had diverted them to Redfern Peak—setting them on a path that would lead them directly to Vale, where the royal soldiers chased them all the way up to the sanctuary gates.

Katerina had never understood her luck. How she'd managed to stay alive. The way the soldiers' arrows fell harmlessly around her, while the others were riddled through and through. How she had landed, perfectly preserved in the snow, while the rest of them had barely managed to crawl out with broken bones and collapsed ribs.

It was like she was charmed. Alwyn had never been trying to kill her. He'd even sent her to the monastery. Kat blinked with realization, knowing her mother's diary was there, encouraging her to unlock her power.

Then somewhere along the line things had changed.

The soldiers who had been chasing them had suddenly aimed to kill. The arrest in Belaria should have taken her life. The river swelled, forcing them towards the deadly Carpathian queen.

Something had changed... but what?

It was like the wizard could read her mind. He nodded slowly, eyes locking with hers.

"Think about it, child." His eyes glowed, willing to her figure it out for herself. "What is the one thing that's held me back all these years? What's the one thing I'd need to set myself free?"

For a second, all was quiet.

Then a chill ran up Katerina's spine.

"Power. All of this... you killing my father, forcing me into exile, sending me on the long journey to the sanctuary. It was all to unlock my power. So that when I came back..."

...you could take it for yourself.

Another shiver ran through the princess and she found herself angling behind Dylan. The plan was as simple as it was ingenious. And she'd walked right into the wizard's hands.

"Your brother's power wasn't progressing as quickly as yours did," the wizard answered quietly, staring at the princess like she was a long-awaited prize. "I suppose, locked away in the comfort of the castle, there was hardly a need. Since Kailas was already a reviled figure—thanks to the workings of my spell—I decided to send you away instead. Hoping the strain of the journey would prompt better results. Hoping your time in the monastery would unlock the secrets of your mother's magic. Unleash the power so I could claim it for myself. And it did."

A manic energy was dancing in his eyes, filling them with an unearthly glow.

"When you laid waste to the soldiers stationed outside Talsing... Katerina, I have never been so proud. I wanted you to come back right then and there. I told Rose to suggest the idea. To fly back to the castle, kill your brother, and burn to the ground everything that was left." He paused suddenly, like a person poised on the edge of a cliff. "However, as fate would have it, you weren't the only Damaris to unlock your power that day."

The entire room turned to stare at the sleeping prince. Hair still dripping blood, hanging limply in his chains. Serafina stood right in front of him, glaring at the wizard with all her might.

"He had no idea what was happening to him," she snarled. "One second we were both just standing there; the next, the entire room was engulfed in flames."

Alwyn burst out laughing again, shaking his head as if the entire thing was just a happy memory. "Don't sell yourself short, my dear. As I recall, the little episode happened only after certain threats against your person were made."

Cassiel took a sudden step forward, looking like some avenging angel of heaven come to life, but Tanya caught him by the arm. Holding him back. Remembering the bewitched dagger.

"But you're right," the wizard continued. "I was able to get something out of him." His gaze rested on a burn on the prince's face, one Katerina hadn't noticed before. "Yes, we were making good progress. That's when I decided that *you*, dear one, were of no more use to me. It's when I stopped trying to protect you and decided to have you killed instead."

She flinched, stung by the casual way he said it. This was coming from the same man who'd sung her lullabies as a child. The man who had taught her how to read.

"Of course, I should have known it wouldn't be that easy," he murmured to himself, eyes sweeping over the entire group, resting on each with thoughtful consideration. "Prophecies don't come by often, and are never to be taken lightly..."

Katerina's head was spinning. The world had tilted on its axis. She had yet to land. Yet the word stuck out like a barb, burrowing in the center of her mind.

"Prophecy?" she repeated, half-wondering why the wizard hadn't just taken her power and killed her already. "What prophecy?"

Alwyn broke out of his thoughtful trance and lifted his head, staring as though he'd entirely forgotten she was there. "*This*—what would you call *this*?" His eyes narrowed with a withering glare, as if she was being very stupid. "What, you thought it was just a coincidence? Talismans of the five kingdoms, it's the five of *you* who come to stand against me? A king of shifters, a queen of men, a priestess of the Kreo, a prince of the Fae, and a vampire consul?"

This time, Katerina wasn't the only one shaken to the core by his words. The others looked around at each other in stunned silence. Some more incredulous than the rest.

"A priestess of the Kreo..." Tanya began hesitantly. "I'm not—"

"My dear, of course you are," Alwyn said briskly. "And it's no wonder, considering who your grandmother is. The only one of you I didn't know until today was the vampire. I had several possibilities but, historically speaking, their kind is so disorganized—"

"What are you *talking* about?" Dylan interrupted harshly. "Just say what you mean, old man."

Katerina flinched preemptively as the wizard's eyes cooled. But he didn't say anything. He simply raised his free hand, pointing all five fingers straight in the air.

There was a quiet gasp of surprise as Dylan's head jerked forward, bending him in a kind of bow. A second later a blur of gold and scarlet ripped from his shirt, flying into the wizard's open hand. It took a second to realize what it was, then Katerina's body stiffened all at once.

My mother's pendant? Why in the world does he want that?

Alwyn's fingers closed around the iridescent jewel, one after another. By the time he had finished, the stone had gone black and cold.

"...protected through grace, as only one can..."

There was a lilting rhythm to the words. Ringing out like a chant, or a verse in a song.

A strange look passed over Katerina's face, and without thinking she reached out and took Dylan's hand. The words were completely unfamiliar, yet she had the strangest feeling that she'd heard them somewhere before.

"What is that—" she started to ask.

But she quickly realized the group had other problems. The wizard had clearly decided the conversational part of the evening had ended. And while Kailas' powers had also begun to progress, he was still out cold. And she was standing right there.

The words fell silent on her lips as the wizard raised his hand. The dagger began to glow.

"I'm sorry to do this, dear one." His hand was steady, but even then his eyes were not unkind. "Truly, it would have been easier if this was Kailas after all."

As if hearing his own name, the prince's body flashed with a momentary glow—the same color as the bewitched dagger. A second later the dagger switched targets, and it was Katerina who was lit with the spectral light. The blade turned slightly, aiming straight for her heart.

"You know, you were always my favorite..."

It was then that several things happened at once.

A distant scream echoed through the chamber. Three pairs of strong hands reached out to pull Katerina back. A flash of color streaked in the air before her. And the princess lifted her head in what felt like slow motion and looked up into Dylan's eyes.

Then there was another scream. Metal clattered to the floor.

Time sped up again as Katerina and the others turned with a gasp. They'd been braced for impact. All of them clustered around the princess, with Dylan standing right in front of her. Turned with his back to the wizard, his eyes on hers, both hands pressed desperately over her heart.

His eyes tightened when he heard the second scream, then widened in confusion. Katerina exhaled with a gasp, and they turned with the others in time to hear a third, furious wail.

It had come from Alwyn.

The wizard was hunched over, clawing viciously at his own shoulders, a torrent of blood spilling down the side of his neck. The enchanted dagger had clattered from his hand, sliding across the length of the room, and it took a second for Katerina to understand what was going on.

For her to recognize the vampire perched upon the wizard's back.

"Aidan!"

He was latched onto Alwyn like an over-aggressive shadow. His mouth was stained with blood, his knuckles were clenched and white, and no matter how violently the man beat at him he maintained a vise-like grip—refusing to let go.

"Run," he managed to say between gritted teeth. "Get the princess, and—"

A flash of neon blue light shot through the dungeon, temporarily blinding the inhabitants, while burning their shadows permanently into the ground. There was a sharp cry, followed by a low impact as Aidan's body flew through the air, smashing into the wall beside the sleeping prince.

He crumpled to the ground and didn't get up. His skin was smoking. His face had turned a frightful white. His eyes were open, but unseeing. As if still trying to process the excruciating pain.

"Cursed vampire scum!" Alwyn snarled, lifting his hands once more and leveling them at the princess. "Not that it matters—I don't need a knife to kill you—"

This time, no one was ready. They were still staring in shock at the fallen vampire. Katerina lifted her gaze and watched with perfect clarity as the wizard fired a shockwave of the same arctic blue in a jagged wave straight towards her. She was still gathering her breath. Still trying to swallow the bitter acid in the back of her throat, when another body threw itself in front of her own.

Katerina barely had time to process. Barely had time to blink as her eyes locked onto the pair staring back at her. One brown, and one blue.

"I'm sorry—"

It was all Rose had time to say. Then the light overtook her, and she fell to the ground.

Dead.

Katerina screamed. Screamed and reached for Rose's fallen body as the wizard went racing forward, illuminated by the strange blue light, that lethal dagger clutched once more in his hand.

There was a deafening bang as the magic folded in on itself. Crumbling and collapsing in a sea of blinding light. The others drew their weapons, then dropped them at the same time—crying out against the bone-crushing force, dazed and reeling, throwing their arms in front of their eyes.

There was a second of silence, the chilling calm before the storm, then the ground they were standing on vanished as they were blasted through the air. Tumbling through the layers of time and space. Ripped painfully from one dimension to another. Screaming and yelling, trying to catch each other's hands. Then finally crashing down into a sea of endless darkness.

The world was quiet once more.

Chapter 3

KATERINA LANDED FACE-down on a slab of flat, hard dirt. Her nose made contact first, and she felt several of the delicate bones break as her mouth flooded with blood. She spat it out quickly and pushed to her feet. Dazed and disoriented. Testing out each limb with the utmost care.

Nothing more appeared to be broken, discounting the sharp abrasions on her hands and knees, but nothing appeared to be quite working either. Her muscles were like gelatin. Her head felt like it had been filled with cold water. Bouts of nausea caused her to buckle and convulse with every step.

"Hello?" she croaked, looking at the empty wasteland around her. It looked like a desert, sun-cracked and covered in sand. "Is anyone there? Hello?"

A dark figure stirred weakly in the distance and she hurled her body towards it. Stumbling and tripping as she went. Coughing out occasional gasps of blood until she reached her destination.

Dylan.

He'd come down just as hard as she had, cratering the dirt around him, wincing as one arm wrapped delicately around his side. His dark hair swirled in the sand as he touched his forehead to the ground, eyes squinted shut, breathing deeply through his mouth. A tremor ran through his body, and for a split-second Katerina thought he was going to be sick. Then he pried open his eyes and focused them slowly on her tall boots. A moment later, they drifted to her face.

"What happened?"

"I don't know," she said immediately, sinking to her knees. The side of her cloak was torn up the side, and already she could see a dark abrasion spreading across her leg. "Are you okay?"

"Where are we?"

"I don't know that either." She gently took his face in her hands, studying his eyes for any signs of deeper injury. "Dylan, are you all right?"

He looked at her in surprise, then glanced down at his body, considering the question. It was like someone had pressed pause. Nothing was moving quite the way he wanted it to. But aside from that, it didn't seem as though there was any permanent damage.

"Yeah, I think so." He slowly got to his feet, unsure whether his legs would actually support him. Then he saw her face. "What about you? Kat, what the heck happened?"

Before she could answer, he gathered her in his arms. Performing the same basic 'damages' check that he'd done a million times before. His eyes tightened with concern, especially when they lingered on her nose and leg, but a few seconds later he released her—temporarily satisfied.

"It must have been Alwyn's magic," he breathed, shivering once in the cold as he gazed out in every direction. "It must have sent us away by mistake. Backfired somehow when it hit—"

His voice cut out as his face went pale. Standing by his side, Katerina cupped a hand over her mouth as her eyes spilled over with tears.

Rose.

She'd half-hoped she'd imagined it. That the beautiful girl was still alive and breathing. That at any moment they were going to find her lying in the sand. But it wasn't meant to be.

The shifter was gone. Her final move of redemption had been her last.

"She saved your life," Dylan said quietly, gazing down at the princess' face. "I know it doesn't erase what she did before, but she saved your—"

"Yeah," Katerina wiped her cheeks quickly, "she saved my life. After my oldest friend tried to kill me. After we sent Aidan away. After I found out that my only brother was under a spell!" Her voice rose in panic with each line, shaking her to the core. Another wave of nausea swept over her and she put her hands on her knees, doubling over at the waist.

"It's okay, you're okay," Dylan soothed, holding back her hair as she retched onto the ground. "Just breathe..."

Katerina tried to do as he said, but the breath just wasn't coming. No matter how much air she gulped in, it's like it wasn't reaching her lungs. It got stuck halfway down her throat. Choking her with the effort. Making the strange desert swim before her eyes.

"Dylan," she gasped, reaching back to grab his hand, "I don't know how to do this. The whole world just... everything just..."

He bowed his head, looking far older than his eighteen years. "...fell apart."

Somehow, just hearing him say it made her stronger. Yes, things were broken. But they were together. They were alive. That's more than a lot of other people could say.

After a few more seconds, she was able to catch her breath. A few seconds after that she straightened up, and together, the two of them gazed out at the desolate place around them.

Under different circumstances, it might have been called beautiful. There was an eerie sort of splendor to the stark emptiness of the land. The straight lines and smooth edges. The pristine isolation. Nothing but miles upon miles of starlit sand.

But to Katerina and Dylan, the place looked like a tomb. A shadowy abyss, with no end in sight and no landmarks to indicate a direction. Not to mention there was no water or food.

"There," Dylan lifted his hand suddenly, his sharp wolf eyes seeing things in the dark that Katerina could not. "Is that...?"

A second later they were both running, as fast as they could manage, over to a crumpled silhouette lying against the horizon. A pale, beautiful man with tangled locks of dark hair. A man who'd saved all their lives, just seconds after they'd turned on him. A man whose eyes were closed.

"*Aidan.*" Katerina sank to her knees, pulling his head up into her lap. Dylan was just a second behind her—reaching out automatically to take the vampire's pulse, then retracting his hand.

"I forgot... no heartbeat."

Instead, he shook the vampire gently. Pulling back his eyelids and checking him over as best he could while Katerina held him steady. She raked her fingers through his black hair—looking for wounds—while Dylan ran his hands up and down each limb, feeling for breaks. When they both came up blank, Dylan leaned forward and started unbuttoning his shirt, hoping to find the cause.

He'd only made it about halfway down Aidan's chest, when the vampire's eyes snapped open and he caught the ranger by the back of the neck. Fangs bared. A vicious snarl piercing the night.

Dylan froze dead still. Either that or the vampire's grip was too strong, and he was unable to move. Either way, he slowly lifted his hands, staring down with wide, starlit eyes.

"It's okay... it's just me."

The snarling stopped, but Aidan didn't release him. Instead, his eyes flashed twice between the ranger and Katerina before he sprang abruptly to his feet, landing several yards away.

"*Just* you," he repeated quietly, the words hissing through the air. He tried to take a step in the opposite direction then froze suddenly, staring down at his trembling legs. Another step and his knees buckled, collapsing him to the ground. "Freakin' A," he moaned, bowing his head to the desert sand just as Dylan had just moments before. "What did we... what happened? Where is this place?"

Katerina and Dylan hurried to catch up to him, helping him slowly to his feet.

"We don't know," the princess said quietly. "Alwyn's magic must have sent us here when he tried to... when he tried to take my power."

...when he killed our friend Rose.

...ex-friend?

...friend.

Aidan thought of her at the same time, and for a second he forgot to be angry and his lovely eyes grew unexpectedly sad. He stared out at the moonlit horizon for a moment, lost in thought.

"I'd hoped that she..." He hesitated deeply, then put it to rest. "She made right in the end."

They were quiet for another moment before the princess stepped forward, putting a hand on his sleeve. "We didn't." Their eyes met. She shook her head, overwhelmed with the atrocity of what they'd done. "Aidan, I can't even begin to..." Tears spilled over and she bit down hard on her lip. "We didn't deserve what you did for us. We didn't deserve you coming back."

He studied her blankly, completely devoid of emotion. "No, you didn't."

They were quiet for a long time. Dylan, staring at the ground. Katerina, quietly crying. And Aidan, staring off into the distance, wishing he was literally anywhere else. Finally, when it became clear there was nothing more to say, the vampire cleared his throat and turned back to the others.

"Have you found anyone else?" he asked quietly, eyes scanning the horizon at the same time.

Dylan shook his head quickly. "No, just you. I was about to shift and—"

"Katerina? Dylan?" a voice called out in the distance, growing more and more hysterical with each pass. "Aidan? Rose? Is anybody there?"

It was Tanya. Kat had never heard her sound so scared.

As one, they left the unfinished conversation behind them—saving it for another day—and moved with a pack-like synchronicity over the endless plane. The pain was excruciating, but they didn't say a word, and they didn't stop moving until they came across a trio of huddled figures.

Cassiel standing with his weight balanced on one leg, holding his frightened sister in his arms. Neither one appeared to be greatly injured, but it was impossible to tell. Tanya was standing in front of them. A gigantic gash ran down the side of her face, as if someone had scraped her from chin to brow with the tip of a knife, but she rushed forward in relief when she saw them.

"Seven hells! We didn't know if you'd made it!" She touched each one in turn, as if proving to herself that they were real. Her eyes brimmed over when she came to Aidan, spilling silently down her cheeks, then she did a quick double-take, looking back over their number. "Where's Rose?" she asked in sudden confusion. "Has no one found her yet?"

In a flash, the six friends split in half. Three of them were waiting with expectation, anxious to hear the news. The other three were blankly staring back, unable to speak.

Of course. They were too far away. They didn't see.

Katerina's heart tightened in her chest as she searched her mind for the right words. Twice she opened her mouth to speak. Twice she came up blank. Eventually, Dylan did it for her.

"Rose didn't make it. She was killed trying to save us from the blast."

Kind of him to say *us*.

In reality, Rose had thrown herself directly in front of Katerina. Trying to shield her from the wizard's dark power. Sacrificing her own life so that the princess might live.

Cassiel stared for a frozen moment, then dropped his eyes to the sand. His arms tightened around Serafina, but he said not a word. Tanya was a slightly different story.

"What... *no*. She was standing right behind me. She never even moved."

"Tan," Dylan said gently, "I'm sorry, but—"

"I'm telling you, you're wrong." Her eyes flashed as she paced past them, searching blindly in the dark. "We just haven't found her yet. We should split up, go in separate directions—"

"Tanya," Cassiel said quietly, never looking up from the ground, "it won't do any good—"

"Stop it! All of you!" she commanded. "Rose is *fine*. She was standing right behind me; she didn't get hit with anything. We just need to..." She trailed off, sucking in a quick breath of air. "I mean, if we can just..."

She took another step into the dark, when a pair of cool hands caught her shoulders. She looked up to see Aidan standing in front of her, staring down with gentle eyes.

He didn't say a word. He simply opened his arms and pulled her closer.

For a split second, she resisted. Then a jagged sob ripped through her body, and she buried her face in his chest. Weeping into his cold skin. Clutching the back of his jacket in little fists.

No one said anything for a long while. They simply stood there in silence, listening to the shifter crying, huddled together in the freezing sand. It was as if a giant hole had been staked right in the center of them. A permanent void they could never hope to fill. Some were bitter, some somber, some enraged. But for the most part, they were simply numb. Too much had happened. There was no time to process it all. They were too exhausted to even try.

Then, after several minutes had passed, a quiet voice spoke up from the dark.

"You didn't find anyone else, did you?"

Katerina looked over in surprise. So much had happened in such a short amount of time, she'd almost completely forgotten there was someone new in their midst. A beautiful young woman, who was staring around the group of friends with wide, hesitant eyes.

Those eyes made a quick pass, then fell upon Katerina.

"Your brother," Serafina said softly, well aware of the gang's animosity towards the prince, but unable to contain the question. "Is he... did he get sent here as well?"

Her voice was quiet, but her eyes were brimming over with tears. The thought of leaving behind the man she loved, tortured and chained, was clearly tearing the beautiful fae to pieces. She waited breathlessly for an answer, silently trembling in her brother's arms.

But it wasn't an answer she was going to get.

"I'm sorry," Tanya snapped, "but what with our friend *dying* and all, the well-being of your beloved prince hasn't exactly been a top priority."

Cassiel's eyes flashed to his girlfriend, but he refused to let go of his sister. Dylan dropped his gaze pointedly to the ground, whilst Aidan merely looked very sad.

Serafina was determined. Sympathetic, thoughtful, but unshakably determined. She flinched at the venom in the girl's voice but stood her ground. More than that, she pushed through the inescapable ring of her brother's arms and took a step forward.

"I'm very sorry for what happened to your friend," she said softly. "I, of all people, know exactly what the wizard is capable of. But did you not hear what he said? Kailas is a victim—like your friend, like all of you. He wasn't in control of the things he did. They weren't his choice."

"But he *did* them," Tanya hissed. She was redirecting—to a massive extent—but at the same time the others could hardly blame her. The death of Rose was one thing, but there wasn't a man, woman, or child in the five kingdoms who didn't know someone who had died by the prince's command. "*Thousands* of people. *Thousands* of lives. *Lost*. All because of your damn boyfriend—"

"It wasn't his choice," Serafina said again, quiet but firm. "It wasn't his fault."

Tanya knew this—in theory. Understood the logic—technically. But she didn't want to hear it, any more than she wanted to respond. Another wave of silent tears rolled down her cheeks as the fae turned instead to Dylan, staring at him with wide, entreating eyes.

"Will you shift?" she asked him. "Run a perimeter, see if you can find his scent?"

There was a slight pause, then an odd expression flickered across his face. "You want me to help you find your boyfriend?"

The second the words left his mouth, it was clear he regretted them. A faint blush heated the tops of his cheekbones and he bowed his head quickly, letting his hair spill down into his face. The fae's eyebrows lifted delicately, but before she could say a word Katerina was quick to jump in.

"He can't shift right now," she said with a bit more force than was necessary. "That fall probably cracked half his ribs. Don't be a martyr, Dylan," she added swiftly, "you know it did."

The silence that followed was even more awkward than before. The others graciously averted their eyes, but Serafina met the princess' gaze with a sympathetic, even friendly, smile.

"If that's true, he'll heal even faster as a wolf. He was probably going to shift anyway."

It was infuriating to be told something new about your own boyfriend by his ex. It was even more infuriating when the girl was genuinely sweet about it. Add on the fact that she looked like some kind of starlit fairytale come to life, and things were pretty much as bad as they could get.

Katerina swallowed hard, then forced a smile just as sweet. "Even if that's the case, I'm sure he doesn't want to. I'm not sure what to believe about my brother, how much he's culpable and how much was out of his hands, but I'm definitely not going to force that opinion on other people."

It was a point well made, but the fae wasn't taking no for an answer. Instead, she turned back to Dylan—trusting just her request would be enough. "Dylan, please. You'll do it, won't you?"

He froze between the two girls, genuinely uncertain, then flashed Katerina an apologetic look. "One way or another, if he's out there we should probably find him..."

As much as she hated to say it, he was right.

Katerina nodded stiffly as Serafina stepped forward and held out her hands, waiting for the ranger's cloak. He undressed as much as was decent, then moved away into the dark to finish the rest by himself. A second later they heard a distant howl, followed by the soft padding of feet.

"Now what?" Tanya asked, wrapping her arms around her chest as she shivered. Her face was still streaked with tears and her cheek was still dripping blood. Her eyes were dark and smudged.

Katerina took one look at her, then sighed. Sitting down in the dirt beside her. Staring out into the darkness. A terrible chill had descended over the moonlit plane. One that seemed to creep inside her skin and work its way down into her very bones.

"Now... we wait."

Chapter 4

DYLAN DIDN'T RETURN for a long time, much longer than was necessary. Katerina suspected he was stalling on purpose, giving himself time to work through everything that had happened. Not that she blamed him. Greatest ally revealed to be greatest enemy? Ex-girlfriend brought back from the dead, only to fall in love with the man who supposedly killed her? She'd need to take some time, too.

In the meantime the moon was rising higher in the sky, and what was probably a scorching desert in the day had sunk to freezing temperatures at night. The friends huddled in a close-knit circle while Katerina shot a wave of liquid fire onto the ground. There was nothing for it to burn, no wood or debris, but these weren't your ordinary flames. They twisted together, then hovered an inch above the ground in a perfect, rotating sphere. Shifting between metallic shades of gold, crimson, orange, and white. Sending occasional showers of sparks crackling into the air.

The others said not a word at the brilliant display of power. They simply moved closer to the heat—stretching out their hands and warming their numbed faces. There was a little gap in their circle, a small space between Aidan and Tanya. At first, Katerina thought the vampire was merely keeping his distance. They had betrayed him, after all. Accused him of treachery. Banished him from their midst. Then she realized who would usually have sat there. Neither Tanya nor Aidan seemed to have realized it was happening, but they were keeping a place for Rose.

"He should be back by now," Tanya finally murmured, breaking the silence. "He should've been back a long time ago. Should someone go out looking for him?"

Cassiel shook his head, looking unspeakably tired as he gazed into the flames. "He'll come back. Just give him some time."

The fae's strong arms were still wrapped around his sister. Now that he'd found her again, he seemed physically incapable of letting her go. They sat posed together like a painting. A sad but beautiful portrait of times gone by. For her part, Serafina seemed perfectly content to be held. In the beginning, she'd been on high alert. Jumping at every sound. Head whipping around with every soft stirring of the breeze. But the longer Dylan stayed gone, the more that hopeful readiness had faded into a dulled sort of resignation. Kailas wasn't out there. If he was, the ranger would have brought him back a long time ago. He was still at the castle with Alwyn, chained to a damp wall.

Katerina fought back a shiver, remembering the dungeon's inescapable chill.

That was the one thing she hadn't allowed herself to think about—her brother.

Between Rose, and Serafina, and Alwyn, there was plenty else to occupy her mind. When the trembling fae had asked that Dylan mount a search, she'd instinctively stood against it. Truth be told, once they'd successfully located the missing three the thought of finding a fourth had never even entered her mind. Even though he was her brother. Even though he was blood.

There was simply no way to process it.

Ever since waking up in the castle all those months ago, staring out the window with that flaming beacon reflecting in her eyes, the princess had been certain of only three things.

My brother killed my father. My brother is a monster. My brother wants me dead.

As she traveled through the countryside, making her way slowly through the five kingdoms, that mantra had been fiercely enforced. There wasn't a creature she'd met along the way that hadn't been personally devastated by her brother. There wasn't a single citizen of the realm who wouldn't give their own life to see him dead. It was one of the few absolutes she had left, and she clung to it with every precarious step. Letting it guide her. Focus her. Motivate her to keep going. There were some nights when she didn't know if she'd make it through without its steadying hand.

And now—even that was gone.

My brother is innocent?

The words didn't sound right in her head. She tried resequencing them. Tried stringing them together in several more palatable ways, trying to ease into the idea. But it didn't work. It stuck out like a jagged piece of glass right in the center of her brain. Disrupting everything that was trying to move around in. Burrowing in deeper with every breath. Creating a slow bleed, one that was quietly but surely tearing her entire life apart.

No, she couldn't think about Kailas.

She couldn't begin to consider his innocence. Not when there were so many other people to consider. So many others' words that made just as little sense in her mind.

Alwyn is the enemy. Rose is a spy.

Correction: was a spy.

How was she supposed to think about her twin, when one of her boon companions had turned out to be working against her? When the man who'd raised her was plotting against her life?

No, she couldn't think about Kailas.

But the longer she sat there, staring at the flames, haunted by images of her brother's pale, emaciated face, the more she could think about nothing else.

At that moment, a distant howl carried over to them on the breeze. The gang looked up in unison, turning their heads in the same direction. If it was an actual wolf, they were either in luck or they were in trouble. Depending on how you wanted to look at it. Depending on how hungry both sides were, and how willing Cassiel was to fight claws and fangs with his bare hands. But there was something familiar about this howl. A few moments later, the outline of a man ventured forth out of the dark. Shaking back his dark hair. Securing his belt without missing a stride.

Whatever damage he'd sustained to his ribs had faded to a dull ache. The slight limp in his leg had been corrected. His calm had returned and banished the tremor in his hands.

Serafina was right, Katerina thought numbly. *He needed to shift.*

He took one look at the fireball, still writhing and whirling like it had a life of its own, before casting the princess a quick look and settling down beside her. He smelled like sand, and salt, and wind. And a great deal of blood. By now, they all smelled of blood. A vague part of the princess wondered how Aidan was keeping himself together.

"There's no sign of Kailas," he said without preamble. This produced next to no reaction from the others. By now, they had all suspected as much. "There are also no landmarks. None whatsoever. I ran for twenty miles in every direction. There's nothing but hills and sand."

Tonight, that wouldn't be a problem. But tomorrow, they'd be needing water. And the vampire would be needing blood. Not that they could begrudge him their own. Not anymore.

Katerina's shoulders fell with a sigh. "I'm too exhausted tonight, but I can try to shift in the morning. With any luck we can figure out where we are, head back to Pora, and—"

"We need to go back to the *castle*," Serafina interrupted suddenly, bright eyes darting around the circle. "There isn't time to waste. Kailas is still in Alwyn's clutches; we need to get him out—"

"And then what?" Tanya demanded. Under most circumstances, she'd probably be trying to play nice with her boyfriend's little sister, but Rose's death seemed to have flipped a switch in her mind. "You saw what Alwyn did to him. That dark smoke. He's still under the wizard's spell!"

"Not always," Serafina vowed. "And it's not as strong as it used to be. He's fighting it. I promise you, he's fighting it." She turned imploringly to the princess. "Katerina, he's your *brother*. I know what you must be feeling, but we need to—"

"No, I don't know if you DO know what she's feeling!" Tanya insisted, her hazel eyes flashing between the streaks of blood dried on her face. "Her *brother* killed her father. Stole her throne. Chased her out of her own kingdom. Set his hell hounds after her!"

"Tanya, that's enough." Dylan's voice carried a warning.

"No, it's not! Why am I the only one who's saying it?!" the shifter cried. "You're not in that dungeon anymore, sweetheart. You need to wake up and think about what you're saying!"

Cassiel's eyes flashed as his arms tightened protectively. That lovely face of his, the one that always had a smile for Tanya, had gone suddenly cold. "Stop shouting at my sister."

Rather than feeling betrayed, the girl was incensed.

"Stop *protecting* her!" Tanya countered. "Going back for Kailas is *crazy* and you know it!" She returned her gaze to the pale girl huddled in his arms. "You remember his *hounds*, don't you—"

There was a blur of action as several people pushed to their feet, standing for the first time against one another, splitting the six friends into even pairs.

The air charged with sudden, dangerous tension, but before anyone could say a single word a quiet voice filtered through the dark.

"Yes, child... I remember his hounds."

The momentum screeched to a halt as the campsite suddenly froze.

Serafina was the only one who hadn't leapt to her feet. She was still sitting exactly where her brother had left her. Her voice, cold and steady. Her ivory skin flickering in the flames.

"I remember them well. The feel of their teeth, the smell of their breath. You speak as if you know them from a story. But I actually remember."

Like peeling back a layer of gauze, the frightened captive suddenly disappeared. That pale, trembling girl vanished into thin air. It was clear to see now—she didn't exist. A steady light shone in Serafina's eyes, and Katerina saw a glimpse of the famed warrior princess who'd fought with Dylan and Cassiel in the great rebellion. The legendary champion who rallied an army to her side.

"When they dragged me to the castle, locked me away in that dungeon, I thought it would only be a matter of time before I made my escape. Before I wreaked vengeance on those who'd imprisoned me. The first time the prince and I met, I tried to gouge out his eyes."

Like looking back through a dream, Katerina remembered the winter's morning she'd noticed two thin scars upon her brother's temples. One day, he'd been unmarked. The next, they were suddenly there. Faint traces of white, so faded they were almost invisible to the naked eye.

"He was my enemy, and I wanted him dead," Serafina said flatly. "There was no hesitation in my mind. Nothing in the world to stop me. For five months, I tried to kill him every chance I got."

While I was upstairs playing cards. Eating pastries. Going riding with my friends. No idea what was going on just a few floors below. Of the girl who'd been imprisoned. Of the wicked darkness taking hold.

"Then day by day, little by little, I began to understand what was going on. To discover that things were not as they had first seemed. By the end of the first year, I no longer saw a cold-blooded killer. I saw a man fighting for his life. A man fighting for the lives of others. Trapped in a wicked game and forced to play the part of the villain. A part he never wanted."

Her eyes leveled with Tanya's, and even thought the shifter had wronged her, even though she'd taken the fae's worst memory and thrown it back in her face, there was no animosity in her eyes. Just a resolved sort of patience. The kind that came from living decades on this earth.

"By Kailas' command, my entire family was murdered. I lost my parents. My sisters." Her eyes flickered to Cassiel, a heartbroken statue sitting in the dark. "I lost my brother. Everything that meant the most to me in the world."

No one said a word, no one dared to breathe.

She pulled in a deep breath, squaring her slender shoulders. "And I forgave him. I even fell in love with him." Her eyes locked with Katerina's. "Because it *wasn't his fault.*"

A profound silence followed her speech. One that resonated in the hearts and minds of every person standing around that fire.

Slowly, they relaxed their positions. Slowly, they settled back down in a circle. No spaces in between this time. All staring at the flames.

"I would have come for you," Cassiel said softly, his long fingers tracing the curve of his sister's hand. "If there had been even a chance that you were alive... we both would have come."

Katerina flashed Dylan a sideways glance through her lashes. He was staring across the fire at the siblings. The look on his face was unreadable, but he nodded silently.

"I know." Serafina bowed her head ever so briefly before twisting around to look at her brother. "And now I'm asking you to. Come back with me. Help me set him free."

The plan was suicide. Absolute suicide. But that didn't seem to matter. At this point, Cassiel seemed ready to do anything his little sister had in mind. He would burn down the world if she asked him to. But in a rare swapping of roles, it was Dylan who tempered the reckless plan.

"One way or another, we're going back to that castle. But it isn't going to be tonight." He was soft but firm, steering them back on course. "We don't have any idea where we are, or who might be looking for us. We're tired and hurt. And Alwyn isn't the sort of man you go up against without a plan. In the meantime, we know he's not going to kill Kailas. Not after he lost Kat."

The fae opened her mouth to protest, but he beat her to it. Holding up a gentle hand.

"*Sera...*" There was a nostalgic tenderness in the way he said her name. A sort of sad sweetness that tugged at the princess' heart. "I promise we'll get him back."

That settled the matter.

At least for the time being.

Without another word, the gang hunkered down as best they could. Nursing torn skin and pulled ligaments. Broken ankles and snapped ribs. They huddled together in a battered little circle as Katerina slowly subdued the fireball to nothing but embers and flickering flames. When she fell asleep, it would vanish entirely. But for now, it chased away the shadows with a steady glow.

One by one, the princess watched as her friends fell into an uneasy sleep. They'd shelved the conversation without saying a lot. A lot that none of them particularly wanted to say. Mainly, how the heck were they supposed to defeat one of the most powerful wizards of all time?

The princess shuddered as she realized that wasn't even the worst of it.

How the heck are we supposed to defeat him once he's taken Kailas' powers?

The thought of the wizard harnessing the dragon was bad enough, but the princess had other questions as well. Ones that swirled like a churning cloud through her tired head, refusing to let her relax. Refusing to let her sleep.

Who were the Kreo? Why did Alwyn think Tanya had some sort of connection to them—a connection the shifter didn't seem to know about herself? What did he mean about there being a vampire consul, and the five of them being talismans of the five kingdoms?

They had met by nothing more than chance.

The fairies had directed her to Dylan, and he'd known Cassiel all his life. They'd quite literally stumbled upon Tanya travelling with a goblin caravan, and Aidan had been assigned as Petra's proxy back at the rebel camp, against his every vehement protest.

At any number of points, the entire consortium could have fallen apart.

What if Cassiel hadn't gone to the festival where they found him? What if Aidan hadn't happened to have been in that bar? What if they'd left just ten minutes later and missed Tanya entirely? What if Dylan had gone with his original instinct and refused Katerina's plea for help?

There was no prophecy. No divine cosmic plan to it all. They'd come together on a whisper and a prayer. And had been holding on for dear life ever since.

And what about my mother's necklace?

Katerina's heart fell as she remembered the way it had grown cold and dark in the wizard's hand. Every bit of beautiful, fiery magic draining right out of it. One of the first memories she had was of playing with the pendant as a child. Eyes dazzled by the spirals of ruby and gold. Batting at it with the chubby hands of a child as it twinkled and danced around her mother's neck.

Now it was gone. That beautiful light extinguished by the wizard's clawed hand.

An unexpected tear slid down the princess' face as she reached up instinctively to touch the place where it used to hang. It was almost as if it had been designed specifically for her. Resting in the little hollow of her throat. Snug and secure. Like it had been carved atop her skin.

Of course, it hadn't been there for quite some time. The day after they met Dylan had demanded it as payment for his services, and had been wearing it ever since. She supposed that she could have asked for it back. After the man pledged his undying love, it wasn't as if he'd deny her a sentimental family heirloom. And she had to admit, she'd never quite gotten used to its absence. The familiar weight. The random blooms of heat. The way it seemed to pulse all by itself—an almost imperceptible rhythm that echoed the beat of her own heart.

And now I'll never feel it again, she thought, lifting her fingers to her throat. *It's lost forever. Lying somewhere on that grimy dungeon floor—*

A soft gasp escaped her lips and her whole body went rigid in surprise.

There, right under the fabric of her blouse, was a small outline—smooth and hard. Her fingers groped blindly at the edges, palsied with disbelief, until she was suddenly sure.

No, she hadn't imagined it. Yes, the pendant was really there. Resting safe against the gentle curve of her neck. As if it had never even left.

"It can't be..." she whispered, and pulled the chain quickly from her cloak, careful not to wake the others. Sure enough, it was her mother's pendant. Looking the same as it had when she was a child. Glowing with an inner fire. Pulsing with that mysterious heat. No longer the deadened black it had turned in Alwyn's hand. It had resurrected. And found its way back to her.

"I thought he took it."

A quiet voice spoke across the flames, and Katerina lifted her head swiftly to see Serafina watching her. She was lying down next to Cassiel—still wrapped safely under one of his overprotective arms—but she didn't appear to have gotten any more sleep than the princess. Her eyes were bright with curiosity as they lingered upon the iridescent stone.

"Alwyn," she said again, as if the princess didn't remember. "I thought he ripped it from Dylan's neck. How did you manage to get it back?"

"I didn't," Katerina replied, still half-frozen with shock. She slipped the chain off her neck and cupped the stone in her hand, rubbing her fingers across the smooth surface. "It's like it just..."

There was a beat of silence.

"...came back?"

The two women locked eyes. Katerina nodded slowly and Serafina softened with a gentle smile.

"It's a powerful magic object," she noted quietly. "I can feel its presence all the way from over here. Those things tend to have a life of their own. And they have a way of getting back to their true owners."

The princess blinked in shock. She'd always thought of the stone as magic, only because it was mysterious and dazzling and she didn't know what else to call it, but she'd never heard anyone else refer to it that way. And Serafina could *feel* its presence? The Fae were more attune to these things than other people, but still. Had Cassiel been able to feel it, too?

"But I'm not its true owner," she said in disbelief, curling her fingers around it and feeling the steady pulse in her hand. "Not anymore. Dylan demanded it in exchange for helping me. I gave it to him months ago and he's owned it ever since—fair and square."

Serafina snorted in laughter. An undignified sound from her dainty mouth. "Dylan *demanded* your jewelry in exchange for saving your life? That sounds like him."

The princess looked up sharply, feeling the need to defend the beautiful man sleeping beside her. "It was before he really knew me. He never would have taken it now—"

"That's not what I'm saying at all." Serafina's eyes danced with amusement. "He obviously saw that it was precious to you—so he took it. To *protect* you. A tether to keep you close." She laughed softly at the incredulous look on the princess' face. "I once saw him ask to hold a hysterical refugee's baby on the entire three-day journey from Ekon to the Vaindroft forest. All to keep the poor mother grounded. On pace, in step. She never once took her eyes off him—not for a second."

In that moment, Katerina remembered suddenly that the beautiful girl had known Dylan a lot longer than she'd known him herself. The two had fought battles together. Lived together. Slept together. Loved each other. Shared the kinds of things that Katerina and Dylan had not.

"It wasn't the same, you know," Serafina said quietly. Katerina looked up again to see the fae watching her, head tilted with a twinkling smile. "What Dylan and I had... it wasn't the same as what you have now."

Katerina wanted very much to accept that at face value. To believe it without hesitation. But it was impossible to look at the breathtaking woman and not imagine the two of them blissfully in love. It was impossible to fathom the weight of the history they shared.

"You don't know that," was what she ended up saying instead. "*I* don't know that."

"But I know him," Serafina said simply. "I've seen the way he looks at you. The way he's always close, hovering around you like you're some sun..." She trailed off with a warm smile. "Dylan Aires has never looked at anyone that way in his entire life."

Katerina smiled in spite of herself. A slow smile that crept up the side of her face. "He's actually going by Dylan Hale now."

Serafina's eyebrows shot up in surprise. For a moment, she was too stunned to speak. Then her eyes rested on the sleeping king with a fierce sort of pride. "He went back? Took up the crown?"

Katerina nodded, glowing with that same pride herself. "He said it was just to get control of the army, but none of us believed that. You should have seen him at the coronation—"

"He did it for you," Serafina surmised. She didn't miss a beat. Just like her brother. "He finally went back to Belaria because of you."

Yes. He'd said as much. However, for whatever reason, it seemed wrong to admit. Boastful.

"He did it for a lot of reasons," Katerina answered evasively, but Serafina wasn't fooled. The old saying was true: it was impossible to hide the truth from a fae. But as she'd come to understand, it *was* possible to derail them. "So you and my brother... you're together?"

A sudden blush spread across the fae's cheeks, and despite how many decades old she might have been she suddenly looked very much like a teenager. "It's difficult to say," she mused, her long white-blonde hair blowing against the sides of her face. "I love him. I know he loves me. So, I guess in that sense, we're together. But I'd only ever seen him through the bars of a cage. I've never held his hand. Walked with him in the sunlight..."

It went suddenly quiet as the two turned away from each other, lost in thought.

Katerina couldn't begin to fathom the depths of what the two must have gone through to fall in love. The years kept apart—just a fingertip away. The endless hours spent in darkness, living and dying by the wizard's hand. How could something so beautiful come from something so dark?

But was it really as beautiful as it seemed?

If it had been Dylan locked in that dungeon, Katerina would have torn the five kingdoms to pieces. She would have set the countryside on fire, just to get him out. She could hardly begrudge the fae for feeling the same way about her own love. Then again, it was nearly impossible to imagine someone feeling that way about *Kailas*.

For years, Katerina had watched that darkness consume him. Taking over, a little bit at a time, until there was nothing left. Nothing she recognized. No trace of her brother left behind.

Could anyone really come back from that? Was redemption reserved for a select few?

"You hate him," Serafina said quietly, as if reading her thoughts. "But you love him at the same time. Deep down. I know you do."

Katerina slipped the pendant back over her head with a quiet sigh. "Yes." She gazed out at the dark horizon. "But I don't know if any of that matters..."

THE TWO GIRLS FELL asleep a little before dawn.

They didn't see the plume of smoke rising in the distance. They didn't see the dots of people peppering the sand along the horizon or hear the distant calls. Their eyes were still closed when the strange green fog drifted over the little campsite, resting a moment on each person, before sneaking inside them with a whispered breath.

They would sleep much longer now. As would the others. They were no longer alone in this strange wasteland, but they didn't realize it at the time. They didn't even notice when they were lifted and carried over the sand. Leaving their campsite far behind them...

Chapter 5

KATERINA WOKE UP SLOWLY. Groggy. As if she'd spent the night drinking too much wine. She couldn't quite feel her body, and it was as if a strange weightlessness had descended over what little she could. Her arms were floating. Her legs were nowhere to be found.

When her head finally cleared she looked up, only to find herself staring into a pair of enormous brown eyes. Eyes that were staring down at her curiously. Eyes surrounded by fur.

"What the heck?"

It was a monkey. A tiny, walnut-colored monkey. The kind with spindly limbs, a disproportionately large head, and gigantic probing eyes. It was perched upon her chest. Staring down as if the princess were something to be studied.

She tilted her head one way, the monkey followed. Tilted it the other, the monkey did the same. She tried to sit up, pushing it gently off her cloak.

That's when the monkey bit her on the nose.

"OW!"

Her shout roused the others. They'd been sleeping and awoke to find themselves in similar states of disorientation. Hair in disarray and legs askew. Scattered haphazardly atop a thick covering of phosphorescent yellow-green moss. It was only then that Katerina forgot the incident with the monkey and realized what was different for the first time.

When she'd closed her eyes that night, everything around her was beige. When she opened them that morning, the world had transformed into an endless sea of green.

The sun-parched desert had disappeared, replaced with a land so soaked in moisture that it pooled in little craters where the princess' elbows dug into the ground. Giant cypress trees stretched as far as the eye could see, making the world bright but shaded at the same time, their branches trailing with translucent curtains of sunlit moss like the tattered sails of a ship. The air was warm and sticky, thick with a perpetual layer of mist that the princess sucked in with every breath. It smelled like moisture, and earth, and something Katerina couldn't identify. Something sweet.

She turned to the others quickly, her ears ringing with the buzz of cicadas.

"What is this place?" she panted breathlessly. "How did we get here?"

Before she could get an answer there was a soft snapping of twigs, and a group of twenty or more people stepped through the trees into the mossy clearing. At a glance, there was nothing overtly unusual about them. It was a standard cross-section, one that you could find in any village. It wasn't until she took a closer look that Katerina saw there was nothing normal about these people at all.

Their skin—a variety of different colors—had all been painted with a swirling series of loops and runes that seemed to cover them from head to toe. Weaving over their bodies like little strands of sap, as if they'd been standing under the trees too long. There wasn't a single one of them that didn't sport at least three piercings (and this wasn't your standard jewelry; these people were pierced with things like gemstones and bone), and despite the fact that they were clearly out in the middle of nowhere not one of them was wearing any shoes.

"Good morning!" A young girl, no older than ten or eleven, stepped forward with a bright smile. "We were hoping you'd wake up before we made it back to the village. Nothing like a first impression, my mother always says. We figured you'd want to walk, instead of being carried."

The friends were stunned. Every one of them frozen in place.

This didn't feel like a kidnapping—they weren't bound, and they were being addressed by a child—and yet they'd clearly been drugged and removed from their camp. This wasn't some sort of a ransom—again, they were being addressed by a child—but they'd lost all their weapons back in the dungeon of the castle and were outnumbered at least three to one. Most importantly, they didn't feel like they were in imminent danger—the moss was cushioning, they'd been left out in the open, and none of them seemed to be harmed—and yet none of them had any idea where they were.

"Tanya," the girl started, clasping her hands behind her back with a grin, and swishing her skirt back and forth, "you probably don't remember me..."

Or maybe... one of them did have an idea.

The others turned in shock to where Tanya was sitting cross-legged upon the moss. A look of unmistakable guilt had flushed her face, mixed with something else—something harder to identify. Despite being as groggy and displaced as the rest, she alone didn't seem at all surprised by their surroundings. She hadn't even blinked when Katerina was bitten by the monkey.

"Gemma?" The guilt vanished as she pushed to her feet incredulously, staring the child up and down. "Is that you? You got so tall! When did that happen?!"

The girl beamed proudly, still swishing her skirt. "Last summer. I shot up four inches. I'm even taller than Joseph now when I stand on my toes."

Tanya snorted. "I bet he loves that..." Then she remembered herself and trailed off, flashing a bashful look at her friends. "Guys, this is..." They had never seen her speechless, but she couldn't seem to get through it. "The thing is, we've somehow ended up..."

The girl, Gemma, walked up to Katerina proudly and stuck out her hand.

"Welcome to the Temple of Bones."

A FEW MINUTES LATER, the six friends were walking through the trees. Sticking close together, feet padding over the soft ground, their wide eyes soaking in every fascinating detail they could find.

The forest—which was actually more of a bayou—was dripping, every inch of it, with life.

Tiny drops of water dripped down from the overhang of trees, though they'd had nothing but sunlight from the time they woke up. A hundred different birds and insects sang together in a huge, discordant chorus. Slick algae sank down into thick mud at the edge of a slow-moving river, curtains of whispering leaves brushed across their faces as they walked beneath, and garlands of flowering vines twisted over every possible surface, filling the air with a sharp, spicy smell.

Katerina jumped back, then stared with fascination as a neon-pink tree frog landed on a fern in front of her, swaying in the breeze and watching her with unblinking violet eyes. She was about to reach out and touch it, when Tanya grabbed her wrist.

"Poison," she said simply. The princess kept her distance.

For another twenty minutes or so, they wandered on a loosely-defined trail through the trees. Long enough that the gang was sweating, their damp hair plastered to the sides of their necks. Katerina understood now why the people escorting them were wearing so few clothes. Not only was it warm, but the air was wet enough that it felt like they were hiking in a sauna. It wasn't long before she slid off her heavy cloak and swung it over her shoulder. The jacket was soon to follow. The men were already down to just their tunics—clinging with perspiration to the muscles of their chests—and seemed on the verge of stripping those off as well.

Rose would have loved it.

A sudden wave of sadness caught Katerina off guard and she pushed it deliberately to the side, turning to Tanya instead. "What is the Temple of Bones?"

It sounded ominous. Like someone saying, 'Welcome to the teahouse of the undead. Please, take off your shoes and make yourselves at home.'

There was a hitch in the shape-shifter's step and she lowered her eyes with a sigh.

"It's a stupid name. There's nothing to worry about," she answered evasively, dodging the heart of the question. "I didn't realize we were so close. I wouldn't have let us—"

"We're here! We're here!" Gemma interrupted with a cheer.

The others looked on in wonder, and Tanya slumped down with a scowl as the curtain of moss parted, and they found themselves stepping into an entirely different world.

It wasn't quite a village, nor was it quite a camp. Katerina didn't know exactly what to call it.

A community. I'd call it a community.

The trees were much larger here and had been strategically culled, making a giant grid-like pattern with plenty of space to walk in between. Whatever structures the community boasted had been carved directly into the ancient wood. The enormous trunks had been meticulously hollowed, petrified over countless decades and worn smooth by the rain. Inside each one, Katerina glimpsed the base of a winding staircase. Steps that were sometimes outside, sometimes in. Stretching high up into the branches where other rooms had been carved into the wood. Rooms where people were eating, or sleeping, or hanging trails of herbs. Where babies were crying, and men were laughing, and birds were flying to and fro—feathering their nests with clumps of moss or bits of twigs.

Each tree was a living, breathing microcosm; home to any of a number of people and creatures. But the trees by themselves weren't enough. Each one was connected to the others by a series of hanging bridges that stretched across the open air. Carefully crafted pathways of rope and wood, not unlike the one Dylan had hacked to pieces back at the sanctuary.

The lower levels looked like shops and store fronts, while the upper levels appeared to be living quarters. Little chimes and dreamcatchers danced and twinkled in the warm breeze, and in the highest branches Katerina could have sworn she saw actual wisps of smoke, where some people had been bold enough to start a fire.

"What *is* this place?" she breathed, too fascinated to be scared. She turned to Cassiel, the person walking beside her. "Have you ever been here before?"

"I've heard of it," he answered, staring around like she was, "never been here. And I had no idea that Tan—" He cut himself off quickly, flashing his girlfriend a silent look.

It was in moments like that, Katerina remembered there was still a lot they didn't know about each other. Her mind flashed to the look on Tanya's face when Alwyn accused her of being some sort of priestess. Dylan's indescribable expression when that crown was lowered onto his head. Her own bewildered surprise upon finding the magical pendant hanging from her neck.

There's a lot we still don't know about ourselves.

The place was bustling with noise when they first entered, but that tapered off very quickly once the villagers registered the group of strangers in their midst. A whispered hush fell over the clearing and the friends proceeded with great caution, following their guides as they wound expertly through the labyrinth of trees. Feeling the eyes of the entire community upon them, peering down from amongst the foliage. Choking silently on the waves of humidity and heat with every step.

Finally, when the tension in the air had become almost unbearable, little Gemma came to an abrupt stop. The group stopped with her, then watched as she skipped ahead and tugged on a hole-ridden blanket resting against a window carved into the side of a tree.

At first, nothing happened. Then there was a disgruntled cough, and Katerina realized it was not a blanket after all, but an elderly woman wrapped in an ancient shawl. She turned around with a grizzled scowl that transformed into a smile when she saw the little girl, bending down to allow the child to whisper in her ear. The smile deepened with a thousand ancient wrinkles, and a second later she lifted a pair of startling bright green eyes across the clearing, coming to rest on the gang.

It was funny, Katerina thought, the way age transformed. And not just its intended victim, but everyone around them. She was standing in a group of six of the most formidable people she had ever met. Kings and princes. Vampires and Fae. Immortal warriors and a dragon to boot.

Yet they found themselves suddenly transformed into a group of nervous teenagers. Taking shallow breaths and fidgeting nervously under the weight of the old woman's eyes.

One person was fidgeting in particular.

"Well, would you look at that. Look who *finally* decided to come home."

The old woman hobbled forward, and Katerina quickly realized her friends were not the most formidable ones there. Tanya seemed to literally deflate under the sudden spotlight but took an obliging step forward, the corners of her lips turning down in a petulant scowl.

"Tanya Calliope Cassiopeia Alexandria Oberon." The others lifted their eyebrows but said not a word as the woman poked Tanya with her cane. "What on *earth* have you done to your hair?"

Every part of the shape-shifter seemed to wince as she turned to the princess and muttered under her breath. "Now would be a really *great* time to see that dragon..."

THE MAGNIFICENT NETWORK of trees was abandoned; whatever quasi-aerial tour Katerina had been hoping for would have to wait. The six friends were led at a comically slow pace to a small hut built from straw and clay at the very edge of the village, trailing along self-consciously as the old woman left deep gouges in the soft earth with the tip of her cane.

The backyard of the hut opened directly onto the water. A part of the river inlet that was no longer moving and had turned into more of a swamp. Waves of heat shimmered above the brackish green, and the princess found herself coming to an instinctual pause as she gazed into the mist.

The water bordering the hut was a wide-open pond, the kind of place where one might go fishing, but it narrowed not far off into a sort of watery pathway. An aquatic trail—wide enough for only a single canoe—that vanished into the mysterious fog that hung over the entire forest.

Katerina wondered where it led. Back to the main river? Or maybe someplace else...

"Hey! You coming?"

The princess jumped in her skin as Dylan's hand came down upon her shoulder. He was staring at her curiously, eyes flickering between her and the swamp, before she ducked quickly under the flap of the tent, face flushing with embarrassment. "Yeah, sorry."

It was like stepping back in time.

The old woman's hut, settled on the bank of a mystical bayou, was exactly the kind of place Katerina and her friends would have imagined when they were younger, playing pretend games and fairytales in the forest behind the castle as their horde of loyal guards and governesses looked on.

It would have been the evil sorceress' lair—it was *perfectly* designed as such. Dirt floors. Clay walls. Strings of herbs hanging from the ceiling. Jars of mysterious, unlabeled concoctions lining the shelves. A fire was roaring in the hearth, even though it wasn't yet noon, and long shadows stretched up the walls as the six friends settled themselves uncomfortably on the floor. It wasn't exactly ideal, but there was nowhere else to sit. At any rate, they were hardly in a position to complain.

"Tanya, brew some tea."

The shape-shifter folded her arms stiffly across her chest. "You know I hate tea. Now, if you had something a little stronger—"

The old woman whirled around, hands on her hips. "And you don't think it's impolite not to offer anything to our guests?"

"...your *guests* are sitting in the mud."

The woman's eyes narrowed. "*Tea. Now.*"

There was something frightfully uncompromising in her tone, and Tanya made the wise decision to obey. While she got up and started rifling through the dried plants the old woman turned back to the others, staring at each with unnerving attention before moving onto the rest.

"In case you hadn't surmised, a group of my people found you sleeping in the desert early this morning. There was no indication as to how you'd gotten there, and they saw that you were without both water and food. They sedated you and brought you back to the village for supplies, and medical attention should any be required."

Aged as she was, it was clear her mind was still sharp. The explanation was quick and efficient. Completely unapologetic whilst holding nothing back.

"Thank you—" Katerina began, but Dylan couldn't help but interrupt.

"We couldn't have come on our own volition?" There was a respectful sort of caution in his eyes when he asked the question, but he still asked. "We were taken by force?"

She met his gaze evenly with her own. "The sedation was for our own protection. Our group included young children, and we take no risks with strangers in these parts." It looked like she was about to say something more, but at that moment there was a quiet knock on the door and the thing tilted open, letting in a crack of sun. "Yes, Samari, what is it?"

A young woman stuck her head in, her wild chestnut curls filling up most of the frame. "I'm sorry to interrupt, Chief Oberon, but you wanted me to tell you when the shipment arrived."

Excuse me? Did she just say...

The friends turned to Tanya at the same time. She'd heated up some water, tossed some leaves in, and plopped back down in the middle of the floor. Now she was staring at the fire, trying very hard to pretend she couldn't feel their probing gazes.

"Chief *Oberon?*" Katerina accused under her breath.

The shape-shifter never blinked. "There's no relation."

"I'm Tanya's grandmother," the old woman announced, concluding her business with the young woman and turning back to the friends with a crooked smile. They, in turn, turned to Tanya, who kept her eyes down and prodded at the wad of congealed leaves floating inside the tea.

"Yeah, except that."

The princess almost laughed aloud. She had precious little experience with the intricacies of family relationships herself, but the dynamic between the two was downright hilarious. There was animosity there. Open animosity. But it was also impossible not to see the strength of their bond.

The threats were plentiful but hollow. The flashing eyes betrayed by an undercurrent of love.

A little smile started spreading up the side of her face, but then Alwyn's words floated back through her mind. *A priestess of the Kreo... and it's no wonder, considering who your grandmother is.* Instead, she turned curiously to the old woman, seeing her in a whole new light.

"*Chief* Oberon?" she asked tentatively. "So that means you're in charge here? These are your people—the Kreo?"

She still had no idea what that meant. She was a princess of the five kingdoms and she had never heard the term until Alwyn said it the day before in the dungeon. Who the Kreo were was a complete mystery to her, as was the fact that her friend would choose to keep her connection to them a secret. Not that she really blamed her. How long had it taken Dylan to admit that he was royalty in disguise? How long had it taken her to admit that she was the missing princess?

We all have our little quirks...

The chief's eyes softened with something close to pity as they fell on the princess. Just like Michael, and Petra, and even Alwyn himself, there was something about the woman that radiated a timeless sort of wisdom. Something about those wrinkled eyes that saw into the princess' very soul.

"You, my dear, have traveled a very long way to ask that question." Her eyes flickered to the rest of the group. "You all have. I can see the journey on you. Hovering like a cloud."

"Seven hells," Tanya mumbled, slumping down beside the fire. "Here she goes..."

The woman's mystical tone vanished at once as she shot her granddaughter a dirty look. "I see you finally found your manners." She gestured to the tea. "Made that all by yourself, did you?"

The shape-shifter jutted up her chin. "I certainly did."

"Your own special little brew?"

The girl sensed a trap and glanced down at the leaves. They'd formed a single, globular mass that had sunk to the bottom of the kettle. "...they were in *your* kitchen."

Her grandmother nodded calmly. Eyes dancing with amusement. "That was kindling, dear. For the fire."

Serafina slowly set her cup down.

"At any rate—yes." The chief turned back to Katerina with an amused smile. "The people here are Kreo, and they are under my care. But I think, my child, that you may be a bit confused as to what exactly that means."

Katerina blushed, but nodded. She had long ago chosen to face up to her ignorance rather than try to hide it and pretend she knew more than she did. It was the only way to get past it. The only way to learn. "I'm sorry, but I am. Are the Kreo shape-shifters?"

The old woman settled down on a tall stool, the only place to sit in the hut. Her eyes sparkled in the light of the fire as she looked down upon her audience. "Some are. Tanya possesses the gift, as do I. We Oberons are one of the oldest shape-shifting lines. However, the word 'Kreo' doesn't refer to a specific type of magic but to a specific type of people. Those gifted with abilities above and beyond what is tolerated by the outside world."

A rather broad category indeed, considering the people sitting in the room.

The ancient woman seemed to read her mind. The wrinkles around her eyes deepened with another smile as she took in the eclectic group. "Yes, the Kreo are made up of all types. We have young witches and warlocks. Aspiring sorcerers and djinns. Shifters who turn into creatures more volatile than what you'd find in the average pack. At one point, we even had a handful of fae," she added, nodding graciously at her guests. "Although they tend to be a bit imperious for our kind."

Katerina stifled a grin as Cassiel and Serafina shrugged in agreement.

"So, yes. The people here are Kreo. And yes, I am their leader. But the Kreo are spread out, encompassing far more than just this one community could accommodate."

The old woman straightened up, pouring herself a cup of the kindling tea. The others watched with morbid fascination as she took a gulp, swished it thoughtfully around in her mouth, then swallowed it down. Whether she remembered what it was or not, it didn't seem to matter.

"The Oberons have been leading Kreo clans for years, and Tanya was supposed to take her place among them," she continued pointedly, pausing for dramatic effect.

Tanya shot a miserable look at the back of her head. The door had opened again, and the poor girl was in the process of having her arms and legs painted in what looked like amber dye. A number of females stood around her, half looked to be trying to hold Tanya down.

"But when her mama passed away, poor thing, she took off."

The shape-shifter shook free of the people attending her with a feral hiss, sending them scattering out the door. "Forgive me for not wanting to live in your little swamp."

"You bite your tongue, young lady!" the old woman thundered before she perked up at some unseen signal, and her eyes fell upon Cassiel with a sudden smile. "But pardon me, I see you've already found someone to bite it for you..."

She sank abruptly to the floor, kneeling beside him. Her arms opened with a grand flourish, and before he could even think to move she took his hand.

"Allow me to introduce myself." Her knobby fingers squeezed around his own. "My name is Lavinia Nicholiana Sombritzia Tagoria Oberon. High Priestess of the Kreo."

The handsome fae froze with surprise, then managed to compose himself enough to shake her hand, offering a polite if nervous smile. "It's a pleasure to meet you. I'm—"

"Silence, child." She pressed a finger against his lips. "I know one of the High Born when he walks into my house." Her eyes swept him leisurely up and down, sparkling with an impish smile. A smile that reminded Katerina strongly of Tanya. "My granddaughter has very good taste." Without further ado, she released his hand and began rolling up the leg of his pants.

"*Granny*!" Tanya shouted, looking absolutely scandalized.

Cassiel pulled back with a start, but before he could say a word the old woman caught him gently by the shin, staring down at his injury from the wizard's enchantment with a critical eye.

"That's definitely a broken ankle," she murmured. Then she ran her hand slowly up towards his knee, fingers curving along the muscles with a toothy smile. "On such a strong, *strong* man..."

Tanya buried her face in her palms. "For crap's sake, Granny."

Cassiel had turned the color of spoilt milk. But for the first time, the others looked like they were truly enjoying themselves. None more so than Dylan, who nudged his friend forward with an encouraging smile. "You know," he said innocently, "I've been told the Kreo are great healers..."

The fae shot him a look that promised certain death, but the old woman was already nodding, snatching up her cane and pushing to her feet. The meeting was apparently over, and the friends were dismissed. All except one.

"We are indeed, and that ankle will have to get fixed. You," she pointed at the group as one. "I've arranged a place for you to rest and change. The entire village comes together for supper every night, and you are all more than welcome." Her eyes then flashed to

the fae. "You, come with me." She hobbled off without a look behind her. "We'll take off those pants of yours and get started."

Serafina snorted and Dylan elbowed her quickly in the ribs,
trying and failing to keep a straight face. As for Cassiel, the fearless
warrior was frozen dead still. Torn between not wanting to offend
his girlfriend's grandmother and not wanting to sleep with her at
the same time.

"She's only joking," Tanya whispered hastily, looking like she
wasn't entirely sure if that was true. "The old bat's got a wretched
sense of humor—"

A croaking voice interrupted them from somewhere amongst
the herbs.

"Come on, beautiful. No need to worry." The old woman
glanced over her shoulder with a brazen wink. "I don't bite...
much."

THE GROUP OF FRIENDS may have vowed to stick with each
other through anything, but that clearly didn't apply to the sexual
advances of a ninety-plus-year-old woman. They brushed off the
fae's silent pleas for help with a cheerful wave and left him in the
hut, walking out together into the bright sunlight. Only one of
them had any doubts. And, ironically enough, it wasn't his girlfriend.

"Are you sure we should just leave him?" Katerina said uneasily,
flashing a look over her shoulder. "Maybe someone should stay behind—"

"Don't worry about it," Dylan answered easily, putting his arm
around her shoulder and steering her back towards the trees. "Cass

can take care of himself. At any rate, they're probably around the same age. A lot closer than he and Tanya..."

The others laughed as they wandered slowly through the maze of trees. Now that they knew roughly where they were and who had brought them, it was easier to appreciate the extraordinary vibrancy of the place around them. It was easier to breathe through the unrelenting heat and admire the community of Kreo for what it was—unparalleled in all its bizarre, eccentric glory.

The trees had emptied out into the shaded clearing, and there were well over a hundred people on the ground. Katerina's eyes travelled from a group of young women levitating what looked like a glowing golden ball between them, to a boy who occasionally sprouted feathers and turned into some kind of parakeet, to an old man who had so many arms the princess thought he was leaning against a particularly complicated root system until he suddenly stood up and walked away.

Multi-colored sparks shot up from a distant fire, raining back onto the dirt in showers of blue and pink and green, and the princess squeezed Dylan's hand with a hidden smile.

This is more like it. I could learn an awful lot here.

It was a testament to the sheer overstimulation of such a place that the group of friends was able to temporarily compartmentalize what had happened to them the previous evening and focus on the moment instead. That, and the brain could absorb only so much trauma before it began trying to diminish it while forcing moments of light.

They wandered about slowly. Leisurely. Soaking in every mesmerizing detail. Panting in the humid air. Basking in the endless sun.

It was probably the most bizarre and diverse group of people Katerina had seen yet.

The only unifying thing among them were those looping, amber tattoos. Even the children had them. Smudged with play, yet carefully drawn around their ankles and wrists. The older people got, the more ink they tended to use. Winding along their limbs and necks. A few of them even sported the tawny spirals on their faces.

And they weren't the only ones...

"*So.*" The princess stopped suddenly in her tracks, turning to Tanya. The girl was sporting some amber lines herself. A few thin patterns her grandmother's minions had been able to draw on before she shook them off. "Is there anything you'd like to tell us?"

The rest of them curved around in a crescent circle, stopping the shifter in her tracks.

"...I'm sorry about the tea?"

Dylan folded his arms across his chest with a pursed-lipped smile. "I thought I was breaking the mold when I took you all to Belaria. But *this*? High Priestess of the Kreo—"

"Stop saying that," Tanya interrupted suddenly. "That's not what I..." She trailed off and stared around the camp.

A pair of twins skipped past, holding hands, probably no more than six years old. Their mop of dark hair scarcely hid the bluish tint to their faces. Or the distinct point to their ears.

"I left this place when I was ten years old. After my mom died, I just couldn't..." A wistful sadness swept over her face before she pushed it away. "I've been wearing different faces of different people ever since. Moving from place to place. Learning to live on my own."

She said it like it was nothing. Like that sort of thing happened to people all the time. She didn't seem to realize how much it said about her. How much it explained.

"It didn't take long out in the real world for me to work up a grudge against the Damaris clan all my own, and by the time you guys found me travelling with those goblins I was finally willing to do something about it. That's it. End of story. No big deal."

A full minute of silence followed her story.

Then Katerina looped her arm around her with an affectionate smile.

"Sure... no big deal."

Chapter 6

KATERINA STOOD IN FRONT of the mirror, staring at her reflection. Gaping was more like it. No matter how many different ways she turned. No matter how many times she tilted up her head or squinted her eyes, she couldn't seem to recognize the girl staring back at her.

When Tanya's grandmother had said there were rooms available for the friends to rest and change for dinner, the princess hadn't given any real thought as to what they might change in to. If she had, she probably would have assumed it was something along the same lines of what she was already wearing. Pants, a shirt. Possibly a dress. Regular clothes.

That notion had been quickly dispelled.

She lifted her arms slowly, staring at the strips of brown leather strapped across her body, clinging to her like a second skin. They certainly didn't cover much, and what they did cover made her look like some kind of an Amazon. A part of her was grateful for the hospitality. Even more so because the place was hot and humid as heck—less clothing seemed to be the name of the game. But another part wanted to faint dead away or hasten to cover herself back up with her cloak.

"How do people even move in this?" she murmured to herself, turning in a slow circle while watching the bands of leather tighten across her chest, watching the tiny skirt cling precariously to her pale legs. "What if everything just... falls out?"

"You learn to get used to it."

Katerina spun around with a gasp as Tanya swung herself gracefully in through the princess' open window. Only the shape-shifter would think it was a fun idea to avoid using the door when they were in a little tree nook a hundred feet up in the air. She was dressed in a similar fashion as Katerina. Her slender body fitted in triangular strips of earth-colored leather that wrapped around her inked skin. Her feet were bare, just like the rest of the Kreo, and the entire outfit combined with her shaved mohawk made her look like some kind of warrior jungle queen.

The princess' eyes widened infinitesimally, wondering if she should quickly acquire a mohawk of her own.

"I don't know if I ever could," she said instead, turning back to the mirror with a slightly worried expression. "And listen, crazy, we've got enough danger in our lives. Learn to use a door."

Tanya grinned and plopped down on the bed. While she may have been initially horrified to find herself back in her childhood home, the longer they stayed the more the place was starting to seep back into her. There was a spring in her step, a light in her eyes, and what looked like a perpetual smile playing around the corners of her mouth.

"Sorry, old habit." She cocked her head to the window. "When we were kids, it used to be a kind of graduation. The day you considered yourself too cool and fearless to use the bridge."

Katerina cast a quick glance over her shoulder. "So we're finally admitting this place wasn't just a pit stop on your way to joining up with our little suicide squad?" she asked coaxingly. "Someone's finally a little glad to be home?"

Tanya flashed her a quick look, froze for a moment, then rolled her eyes and pushed briskly off the bed. A second later she was standing behind Katerina in the mirror, picking up strands of her long red hair. "I told my granny what was happening back at the castle. About the rebellion and the armies. About who's really been pulling the strings." Almost absentmindedly, she began braiding random locks of the princess' hair. Fingers blurring with practiced speed. "She won't help us. Says the Kreo don't get involved. Kind of like Michael back at the sanctuary."

Katerina kept a straight face, but her heart fell. Truth be told, she hadn't been expecting the villagers to pledge people of their own. There weren't many to begin with, and those who were the right age to fight probably had no idea how. Still, having just seen the kind of firepower they were up against, it was hard not to crave all the help they could possibly get.

"That's fine. They're helping already," she said quickly, eyeing the stoic expression on Tanya's face. "They brought us out of the desert, they're giving us shelter and food."

"It's not enough." The shape-shifter spoke quietly, but her face had twisted with an angry scowl. "The people here are despised throughout the five kingdoms just for being born with what others weren't. They've been persecuted to the point of isolation. Completely cut off from the outside world. Now a chance comes for them to change all that, and they won't stand up and fight?"

Her fingers were flying so fast, Katerina was having a hard time keeping track of them. All she felt was the occasional gentle tug as her wavy curls were laced with ribbons of braids.

"It's one of the reasons I left," Tanya continued softly. "This place used to be thriving. A major trading port on the river. Now, it's a virtual hermitage."

She dropped her hands suddenly, finished with Katerina's hair, and the princess took a moment to gawk at the finished effect. She'd wanted to look more gladiatorial like Tanya? Well, mission accomplished. Between the hair and the clothes, there was a rugged edge to her now. An air of danger and defiance. With a secret grin, she slipped off her shoes.

"It's home, Tanya." She turned around to face her, resisting the urge to give the standoffish shifter an unwelcome hug. "You think I like where I come from? Doesn't matter; it's still home."

A faint grin drifted across the shifter's face as she glanced around.

"That's right. The good ol' bog."

Katerina snorted, following her gaze. "Why do they call it the Temple of Bones, anyway? I was looking around all day, but there's no temple."

"Like I said, it's a stupid name." Without a backwards glance Tanya hopped back onto the windowsill, preparing to make her jump. "You coming? Or is someone still using the stairs?"

The princess ignored the jab, feeling suddenly serious as a question floated to the surface of her mind. "Tanya... if you're really some kind of Kreo priestess like Alwyn said—"

"I'm not," the shifter interrupted firmly. "I left that life behind."

"But if you *were*," Katerina pressed, unwilling to dwell on semantics when there was so much more at stake. "...do you think there could also be a prophecy?"

A guarded expression stole across Tanya's face, and Katerina knew she wasn't the only one preoccupied with the question. Odds were, the entire gang had been able to think of little else. They were quiet for a minute before the shifter turned back to the window with a sigh.

"I don't know, Kat. I don't know."

IT WAS EASY ENOUGH to find the feast that night. The ground was lit up with a blinding array of torches, and everyone in the village was making their way boisterously down to the same spot. It was much more difficult trying to find Dylan's room.

All Katerina had been told was 'he's in the same tree.' When you were currently staying in a two-hundred-foot enchanted cypress, that left a bit more to interpretation than one might think.

She had already burst in on three unsuspecting strangers (two of whom were engaged in a pre-feast celebration all of their own), and was about to give up entirely, when a familiar voice floated out of a torch-lit window about ten feet above her head. Choosing to abandon common sense in an effort to impress her boyfriend, she secured a good grip on the branches and pulled herself up, leaving the safety of the bridge behind.

Don't look down, she told herself. A second later, *Crap! Why'd I look down?!*

After dangling there for a good thirty seconds, too scared to move but too embarrassed to jump back down, the princess forced herself to keep climbing. Just a few seconds after that she was heaving herself breathlessly onto the window ledge, thanking the gods of bad decisions that she hadn't plunged to her death and vowing never again to 'graduate' like Tanya Oberon.

It should have been a comically disastrous ending to her would-be impressive move. She'd imagined herself perching lightly upon the window sill, clearing her throat and tossing back her long hair like the jungle warrior she was. Not spilling awkwardly—legs tangled, panting, sweating, and breathless—into the middle of the floor.

But as the fates would have it, she got a free pass. She might have fallen, but Dylan didn't notice her right away. He was having problems of his own.

"How the *heck* is this supposed to work?"

In the ultimate irony he was standing in front of his own mirror, just as she had been. A look of profound frustration creased his handsome face as he twisted to and fro, jaw clenched shut, desperately trying to figure out the complicated leather straps that held his shirt together. Every time he tied one down, another would pop up. Every time he got that one under control, two more would somehow take their place. He looked like he was on the verge of just cutting them off altogether, when someone softly cleared her throat behind him and he spun around with a start.

Katerina was sitting casually on the window sill. Hair fixed, clothes straightened, and smirking as though she hadn't just fallen and happened to swing around in trees all the time.

"*Kat*," Dylan gasped in surprise.

She smiled languidly. "Having trouble?"

A bright flush spread across his face as he glanced self-consciously down at his body. By now, the shirt was clearly inside out and all his attempts to fix it were only making it worse. The pants were easy enough, hanging low on his hips, but he'd obviously given up on the decorative cuffs meant to go around his wrists. The optional headband had also been discarded.

It was beyond cute.

Katerina didn't think the guy had ever been physically self-conscious in his life, and he clearly didn't know how to handle it now. After a few failed attempts to speak, he simply crossed his arms over his chest—trying to shield as much from view as possible. Of course, he still denied it.

"...no."

Defiant till the end. That's my man.

For a moment, the two simply stared at each other. One with a caustically raised eyebrow, the other stubbornly lifting his chin. Then Katerina burst out laughing and leapt down from the window, crossing over to join him by the mirror.

"I had the same trouble with mine," she said graciously, still grinning as she spun him back around and started fiddling with the straps. "These things they wear are ridiculous."

Truth be told, it was a bit hard to focus. The sight of Dylan on a 'bad day' was tantalizing enough. She didn't know what to make of this sweaty, jungle version of him.

"Ridiculous..." he repeated breathlessly. She glanced up and realized he was no longer concerned with his own reflection. He was staring wide-eyed at her. "...*not* the word I would use."

Looks like I'm not the only one who can't focus.

A second later he abandoned the mirror entirely and turned to face her, slipping his arms around her waist and pulling her closer with a little grin. His fingers grazed the bare skin of her ribcage, slowly exploring everything that would usually have been covered before winding along to the small of her back. They came to rest teasingly on the top of her skirt.

"Not the word I would use at all."

There was a quiet hunger in his voice. A hunger that shimmered deep in his eyes and sent shivers racing along Katerina's skin. All the 'cool points' she'd racked up by the window disappeared as her legs turned to jelly and she found herself suddenly unable to breathe.

"Oh yeah?" She tried desperately to keep a handle on herself, wrapping her arms lightly around his neck. "What word would you use?"

His hair was damp, and his skin was steamed from the moisture coming in from outside. It glistened on the muscles on his arms and chest, even more so when the last stubborn strap gave way and the shirt fell off him entirely. He took a step forward, closing the gap between them. Skin pressed up against bare skin as he lowered his head and stared down into her eyes.

"*Mine.*"

She was off her feet before she could answer. Swinging wildly through the air before he shoved her roughly against the wall. Her legs circled around his waist of their own accord as his strong hands wrapped around her thighs. She opened her mouth with a gasp but his lips closed over hers, absorbing the sound into himself.

The smell of him was everywhere. The heat of him was everywhere. His body pressed hard against hers as his fingers tangled furiously in the braids running through her hair.

A sort of electric buzz swept through her, setting her blood afire as her nerves jumped and danced. A low moan escaped her lips and the kiss deepened. His tongue was in her mouth. He tasted spicy and sweet, with the faintest hint of ale. She pulled on every bit of him she could reach. Scratching her nails down his back. Tightening her legs around his hips. Anything to get him closer.

It wasn't until his hand went up her skirt that the two of them suddenly stopped.

"What is it?" she whispered, panting for breath.

It was he who had pulled back, not her. She was perfectly willing to keep going. Perfectly willing to skip the feast entirely and see what mischief they could get up to instead. But Dylan had frozen perfectly still. His lips parted in surprise. His eyes locked on her neck.

A second later he caught the golden chain between two fingers, staring up at her in shock.

"How do you have this?"

There was a hitch in Katerina's breathing as her racing heart finally slowed. She hadn't been trying to keep it a secret. But between being kidnapped from the desert and carried into the jungle oasis only to be served foliage tea, it had completely slipped her mind.

"I don't know." She loosened her legs from his waist, sliding gently to the floor. "I woke up with it hanging around my neck. I didn't try to take it back from Alwyn. I actually thought that he'd broken it forever when it turned black in his hands."

It certainly wasn't black now. It was glowing as brightly as she'd ever seen it. Waves of gold and crimson fire spinning furiously around its enchanted core.

The color sparked in Dylan's eyes as he looked up at her in wonder. "It just... came back?"

She nodded silently, reaching up to run her fingers along the smooth stone. While she could feel it was technically hot to the touch, it felt cool against her skin. Cool and strangely reassuring.

"Serafina said that magical objects tend to return to their original owners, and that the pendant has a strong magical pull. She said she could feel it all the way across the fire."

If it was possible, Dylan looked even more surprised. "You talked with Sera about it?"

It was like flipping a switch. The second he said the name, all that raging hormonal fire in Katerina suddenly cooled. It was impossible to think about what they'd been about to do without remembering that he'd already done it with Cassiel's beautiful sister.

That while every moment might have been a first for her, it was by no means a first for him.

"Uh, yeah..." She ducked casually out from beneath his arms. "I did." Well aware that he was watching her every move she hastened to compose herself, smoothing her clothes and trying to subdue the wild mess of her hair. "At any rate, I just came to get you for the feast—"

"Kat... what's wrong?" He quickly crossed the space between them, staring down with a worried crease between his eyes. "Did I say something—"

"No, not at all." She brushed him off quickly. "I'm just really hungry—"

"Okay, did I *do* something?" he pressed, ignoring her pathetic attempts to flee. When she didn't answer, his face went suddenly pale. "Katerina, if that was moving too fast, I would never—"

"What are we supposed to do about Alwyn?"

If hearing Serafina's name was enough to eliminate her sex drive, hearing Alwyn's was most certainly enough to do away with his.

His face whitened another shade as he took a step back, raking his fingers though his sweaty hair. "I have no idea what to do about Alwyn."

This from the man with an answer for everything. The man who always knew the next step.

It should have scared her, but in a way she was almost happy to hear him say it. Relieved to see that she wasn't the only one who felt like the very ground she'd been standing on had been ripped away. Traces of panic bordering on hysteria were layered just below the surface of Dylan's sky-blue eyes, and no matter how hard he tried to control it that same panic tightened the edges of his voice.

"It was bad enough when we were going to be fighting your brother," he admitted. "I had no idea how you were going to react to something like that. What it would do to you when it came down to that final moment. But I always thought we could win," he added suddenly. "With our forces against Kailas, I always thought we could win. Now... I'm not sure what I think."

Katerina sank down onto the bed. The bed that was looking entirely different now than it had just a few heated moments before. "But does it really change our plan? I mean, we're gathering all the people we possibly can to march on the castle. We have all the rebel camps, whatever grass roots movement we started with that midnight flight, and Belaria's entire army—"

"Against a *wizard*."

Just one small word, but they both knew it was enough. There was no telling what Alwyn might be capable of. Especially if he succeeded in stealing Kailas' power.

They were quiet a long time, sitting side by side on the bed, before Katerina finally spoke.

"My brother..." she began softly, hardly daring to look Dylan in the eyes. "You know I can't just leave him down there. Whether he was under a spell or not... I can't just leave him."

Dylan's body tightened for a moment before it relaxed with a sigh. "Yeah... I know."

THE FEAST WAS EVERYTHING it promised and so much more. Even though Katerina and Dylan sat down together with heavy hearts, it was impossible to stay that way in the heat of the moment.

The night was lit up with a rainbow assortment of pixies, fairies, and magically-fueled torches. A massive bonfire roared and sparked in the middle of the clearing while scores of spirited musicians danced around the flames, growing louder and more out of tune the more they drank.

Dozens of tables had been set up beneath the stars. Tables groaning under the weight of so much food, Katerina had no idea how the entire village could possibly manage it. There were breads, and meats, and fruits, and a strange fish-like substance that the princess had never seen before but knew instinctively to avoid. On top of that, there were cakes, and crèmes, and desserts.

But more than anything, there was whiskey.

"So this is where Tanya got it," Dylan murmured into Katerina's ear, nodding with a grateful smile as a passing warlock poured him another drink.

Katerina leaned up against him, her head already spinning. "Got what?"

"A tolerance as high as mine."

The princess giggled and glanced at the others seated around the table.

Aidan was in fine spirits, drinking a mixture of blood and ale while what looked like some kind of leprechaun tried to read his fortune. Tanya had fully regressed back into her childhood home and was loudly regaling all those within earshot of her grand adventures on the road. Adventures that mostly seemed to consist of the others getting themselves into trouble, and her repeatedly saving the day. Cassiel had finally been released from 'Granny's clutches'—although he refused to talk about what had actually happened—and was sitting with his sister.

And Serafina was actually having a bit of a hard time.

"Just try to eat a few more bites," her brother coaxed quietly, stabbing around on her plate with his own fork. "Just a few more bites, then I'll take you back to the room. I promise."

Katerina's smile faded as she and Dylan looked over at the same time. Food hadn't been exactly plentiful the last two years living down in the dungeon, and the fae's delicate body was having trouble processing it now. While she was slender to the point of emaciation she seemed to have lost any semblance of an appetite, and the sight of the feast was making her feel sick.

"That's what you said a few bites ago," she teased, but her voice was strained. "Just let it go, Cass. I'm fine. I'll see you in the morning."

She tried to push to her feet but his arm tightened around her shoulders, easing her back down onto the bench. "I would be happy to let you leave... as soon as you eat a few more bites."

Her body wilted with a sigh and she shot him a look of sisterly exasperation. Whatever troubles she was having clearly weren't helped by the fact that his arm was permanently embedded around her shoulder. Not that there was much she could do about it at the moment.

"You know," she picked up a butter knife and stabbed it viciously into a biscuit, narrowly missing his fingers in the process, "you're going to have to let go of me at some point."

"At some point," he agreed absentmindedly, then gave her a sweet smile. "In the meantime, you're going to eat that entire biscuit."

Dylan winced sympathetically, watching them by Katerina's side. "I was once held for twenty days by a Vengosi caravan for beating their driver at cards. When you get out, food is the very last thing on your mind." His eyes tightened, and he gestured with his head. "Do you mind if I..."

"No, go ahead." Katerina stood up quickly to let him pass. "I think I'm going to look around for a little bit anyway."

She didn't know how many nights they were going to spend with the Kreo. She didn't know how many nights they had left, period. But she wasn't going to waste a single one.

Taking her glass of wine with her, she got up from the table and started wandering in an aimless circle through the raucous party. Every direction she looked, things were more fantastical than the last. From strings of airborne pixies dancing a traditional waltz, to an impromptu fistfight between two upstart youths (one of whom was quickly sprouting antlers), to the sonorous wailing of a trio of witches who had taken up singing with the band.

Each sight burned into the princess' eyes. Becoming engraved into her very soul.

These were the people who would suffer if she were to lose this fight. The little hermitage would continue to diminish, until there was nothing left. Their magic, so precious and unique, would be ripe for the taking. And she knew a wizard who would jump at the opportunity.

Alwyn wasn't a man of the people. He didn't just want to take down the Damaris line. He wanted power—plain and simple.

Her mindless wandering had taken her in a slow circle all the way around to the back of the village. The wineglass was empty now, and she found herself standing all alone in front of the chief's tiny hut. The party still raged on just a short way away, but where she was standing things were peaceful. Quiet. So quiet she could hear the hum of the fireflies drifting over the warm breeze.

I should get back, she thought. *Don't want anyone to worry.*

But even as she thought the words, her eyes drifted without permission past the little hut to the swamp that lay just beyond. Not a single ripple disturbed the green water. It was as smooth as glass. A thick layer of mist hovered an inch above the top, almost obscuring the narrow waterway that vanished out into the trees, but Katerina knew it was there.

And she had a sudden, overwhelming impulse to get closer.

Casting a quick look over her shoulder, she set down her glass where she stood and scrambled down the slick, algae-covered bank to the shore. She was wrong about it being a good place to go fishing. The mud was thick as quicksand, sucking at her feet and leaving her no place to safely stand. She was about to go back, join the rest of the party, when her eyes caught sight of a little boat tied to a plank of wood a few feet out from shore.

Don't be stupid. It's not your boat, and why the heck would you even go?

One day, Katerina was going to learn to listen to that voice inside her head. The one always prompting her to stay out of trouble.

But today was not that day.

Without stopping to think she worked her way quickly to the rope, her bare feet leaving deep gouges in the mud. She tugged hard on the end, and a second later the boat was moving slowly towards her through the water, silently pushing its way through a layer of green slime.

It was more of a canoe than anything else. Room enough for a single person. Katerina climbed inside the second she was close enough, located a paddle and pushed hard away from shore, pointing the wooden nose into the curtain of mist.

The cloud parted silently before her, then quickly closed again behind. Swallowing any trace of the little boat as she slowly made her way across the brackish pond. The air was even thicker over the water, and the sound of cicadas drowned out any noise from the party. Her ears were ringing with it and her skin was covered in clammy goosebumps despite the evening heat.

Each time she opened her mouth, it was like breathing underwater. Her arms and legs were sticky, and tendrils of auburn hair clung to the sides of her neck. She was perfectly alone, much more so than she'd been at any other point in the last few months, and yet she couldn't shake the feeling that she was somehow being watched. Her eyes darted back and forth, trying to pierce the impenetrable fog, and she quickened the strokes of her paddle.

Just a few seconds later, her efforts were rewarded. The water narrowed suddenly into a little stream, one that moved with a current of its own. The princess put the paddle down and leaned back as the canoe was swept along of its own accord, moving at a brisk pace over the waves. To the left and right, she saw the same kind of foliage they'd been hiking through earlier that day. For a second, she even thought she could glimpse the same trail they'd come in on. But before she could be sure, the canoe struck something hard beneath the water and she was thrown forward.

"Crap!"

She caught herself on the rim of the boat, just barely, and lifted her eyes in wonder. It was a tree. That's what had stopped her. But it was a tree unlike any she'd ever seen before.

The branches weren't the same uniform green as everything else in the bayou; they shone with an iridescent shade of silver. An unearthly shimmering hue that looked completely out of place yet felt completely natural at the same time. Although a breeze had picked up, rustling through the rest of the forest, the branches of this tree stood perfectly still. Not a single flutter of its silver leaves.

The roots stretched all the way down to the water, and even as Katerina leaned over the side of the canoe for a closer look she noticed a strange hum coming off the wood.

Not the hum of birds or insects. Not even the faint rushing sound of the water as it swirled past the canoe. This sound was different, but eerily familiar.

It took Katerina a second to realize what it sounded like.

Voices.

Her eyes widened as she stared up at the moonlit branches. Now that she'd recognized it, there was no mistaking the sound. It was voices. And they were coming from inside the tree.

Hands trembling, she grabbed the sides of the boat and slowly lowered a foot to the shore. She was only about an inch or so away, when she suddenly froze. Torn with indecision.

What am I doing here? And why would I get out of the boat?

She had no idea how much time passed as she hovered there, debating what to do. It could have been seconds, it could have been minutes. All she knew was that her fingers clenched around the railing had already begun to go numb with the pressure, when something about the muddy shoreline suddenly caught her eye. Something she couldn't believe she'd missed before.

There was already a set of tracks.

"Well, well, well..."

Katerina looked up with a gasp as a shadowy figure walked out of the mist.

"I was wondering when you were going to show up."

Chapter 7

IT WAS A GOOD THING the water was so shallow. It made things a lot easier when Katerina fell out of the boat.

"Yeep!" She made a noise somewhere between a screech and a cough, landing with an undignified splash in the brackish water. Smears of algae billowed across her skin as a rush of what tasted like raw sewage poured down her throat. She spluttered and flailed, then surfaced just a moment later, spitting out a disgusting mouthful as her hands and feet planted in the mud.

It was bad enough without the slow applause that followed.

"A magnificent performance! But I would work a little on the landing."

Story of my life.

The princess looked up with a watery glare at the old woman standing before her. She would have hardly recognized Tanya's grandmother—relieved of her usual tattered shawl—but the frog skull mounted atop her piles of grey hair was a dead giveaway. And a terrible fashion statement.

"I aim to impress," Katerina answered sarcastically, pushing with some difficulty to her feet and slogging forward through the mud.

How the heck did she get out here anyway? I took the only boat.

"So... I see you found it." Chief Oberon gestured up to the silver branches haloed around them, stretching up to the stars. "I knew you would. Saw you looking when you came to visit me earlier this afternoon. Once the pathway catches your eye, there's no resisting its influence."

There was something unsettling but strangely reassuring about the old woman all at the same time. A kind of duality that left her one part wrinkled old grandmother, and one part all-powerful shape-shifting priestess of the Kreo. Neither one was to be taken lightly.

"I found... what, exactly?" Katerina took a step forward onto solid ground, gazing up at the shimmering leaves. She could still hear the hum of voices but it was softer now, like they'd fallen behind a veil.

"The tree of truth." The old woman looked up fondly, as if she'd personally had a hand in growing it. "People come here for answers. Answers to questions they didn't even know they had."

The pendant pulsed hot against Katerina's skin and she took a step closer, laying her hand against the smooth bark. She could almost hear them. Almost make out what they were saying.

Almost.

"I don't understand," she began, the logical portion of her brain rebelling against the idea of an existential tree. "How does—"

"It's not for you to understand," the old woman interrupted kindly. "It's simply here for you to experience. Open your mind, princess, and relax your body. The answers will come."

Right now? With you watching?

There was a pause.

...apparently so.

Katerina tried to do as she asked. She sincerely did. But it wasn't so simple.

Her legs still ached from when she'd hiked through the jungle. Her head was still spinning with the wine. Her lips were still bruised where Dylan's teeth had sunk into them, and her skin was still covered in a layer of disgusting, green slime.

She wiped it away from her face with a grimace, distracted by the smell but trying her best to meditate, her fingers brushing against her mother's delicate gold chain.

"Now where in the seven hells did you get something like that?"

Her eyes shot open again to see the grizzled Kreo chief looking at her with nothing short of astonishment. She was much closer than where she'd been standing just a moment before, her bright eyes dancing with the light reflecting off the fiery pendant.

Katerina quickly closed her fingers around the stone. Feeling abruptly protective. "It was my mother's. She passed it on to me."

Much to her surprise, the old woman chuckled. She flicked a gnarled finger at the glittering jewel before leaning back against the tree. "And it seems very happy that she did."

...happy?

Katerina glanced reflexively down at the necklace before lifting her eyes with a cautious stare. Between the frog skull and the general moth-bitten attire, there had been no concrete proof that the woman wasn't at least a little bit unhinged. This could seal the deal—right here.

"It does?" she asked with a bit of a smile. "You think it seems happy it was passed to me?"

"And why wouldn't it be?" the woman asked matter-of-factly. "I would be, too, if the only other option was your brother."

"No, I meant..." Katerina was about to say the obvious. About to comment on the fact that, while the necklace might be beautiful, it couldn't exactly *feel*. But even as she was about to say them, the words froze suddenly in her throat.

The water had called her to this place, the tree was whispering her name... why wouldn't the pendant possess the capacity to feel? Nothing in this world was ever quite as it seemed.

She remembered what Petra had told her, about the day the rebel commander had given the pendant to Adelaide Grey. 'I did it to help her,' she'd said. 'A light to guide her way.'

A light to guide her way...

Katerina's fingers closed around the jewel with a silent gasp. Feeling the steady pulse against her fingers as a sudden truth opened up before her. One that had been right in front of her eyes.

The pendant dulled when she'd first left the castle—because her place was on the throne.

It had glowed when she gave it to Dylan—because he was meant to be in her life.

It had burned red-hot when the two of them kissed—because they'd fallen in love.

And it had turned black and cold in Alwyn's hand—because he was never meant to have it.

It's literally a guide, she thought in astonishment. *To keep me on the right path, keep me from making bad decisions. A light to guide my way.*

The entire realization had taken only a few seconds, but she might as well have been speaking out loud. When she looked up the old woman's eyes were still upon her, glowing with satisfaction as the princess gave her a tentative smile.

"Tree of truth, huh?"

Oberon gave a rasping cackle, one that was warm despite sounding like dried leaves. She peeled herself off the trunk, hobbling forward to examine the necklace for herself.

"The only one of its kind." She ran a finger appreciatively over the stone. "Think of it as a sort of gateway, channeling the wisdom of previous generations."

Katerina shook her head in amazement, a bit overwhelmed by what had just happened. "I just can't believe it," she murmured. "All this time, I thought it was just a pendant."

"A pendant?" The old woman leaned back on her heels, looking amused. "Well, it isn't that either, dearie. It's an amulet."

Katerina blanked. "An amulet?"

The old woman nodded sagely. "Meant for protection."

The confusion tripled.

"*Protection?*"

The word jarred something in the back of the princess' mind, but no matter how hard she tried to remember it hovered just out of reach. Like the voices, whispering back and forth in the silver leaves. She was still standing there, frozen in a sort of trance, when the old woman stepped forward and patted her kindly on the back.

"I don't envy you, Katerina Damaris. It's a lot to be placed on the shoulders of one so young. But have faith—we are never given more than we are strong enough to handle."

Their eyes met, and the woman gave her a wrinkled smile.

"You may even surprise yourself."

The enchanted stone glowed warm against the princess' neck and her fingers curled around it, hoping very much that it was true. Hoping very much that the world would stop spinning long enough for her to secure a hold. Hoping very much that she could find a way to defeat the darkness set against her. That she wouldn't let her mother down.

It wasn't until the breeze picked up suddenly around her that Katerina realized she was standing alone beneath the tree. Chief Oberon was gone. She wondered if she was ever really there.

THE PARTY RAGED ON long into the night, growing louder and louder as the moon made a slow orbit across the sky. But the princess wasn't there to see it. With a look of deep inner contemplation, she'd settled herself beneath the branches of the silver tree. Leaning back against the smooth bark, letting the leaves brush against her face, listening to the quiet whisper of voices floating in the air.

She hadn't planned on staying, but she was in no particular hurry to leave. Quite the contrary, she felt as though she'd strayed outside the stringent reaches of time.

The air was warm and pleasant. The quiet water moved at a slow pace. For longer than she even realized, she sat beneath the moonlit branches. Thinking. Remembering. Closing her eyes and letting her mind wander as her mother's amulet glowed like liquid fire in her hand.

Protection. The amulet is meant for protection.

Again and again she replayed the words in her mind. Considering them from every possible angle as she tried to piece together what she was missing. Tried to find the memory that was lost.

Funny that Alwyn would have let me double back to my room the night my father died just to let me retrieve it. But, then again, it wasn't until recently that he actually wanted me dead—

Her eyes snapped open in mid-thought. Like someone had hit her over the back of the head.

Alwyn.

That's what was so familiar about the word. Why it sounded so strange yet pressing in her ears. He was the one who'd said it. Back in the dungeon, seconds before he blew them all away.

Like finally remembering a dream, the words echoed back to her...

"...*protected through grace, as only one can...*"

"That's it!" She pushed to her feet, pale as a ghost, yet lit up and smiling. "That's—"

A low growl cut through the quiet, raising the hair on the back of her neck. A second later the ferns parted, and it was followed by a shadow of black fur, a pair of glowing yellow eyes.

It was only then that Katerina realized what had been following her since she set off down the river. It was only then she realized she hadn't been imagining the feel of hidden eyes.

She stood perfectly frozen as the panther walked out onto the shoreline. Crouched to spring on the other side of the river. Their eyes met, and for a moment the world stood still.

"Alwyn." She dropped her hands to her sides. "I liked you better as a raven."

Chapter 8

THERE WAS NO TIME FOR brave words or witty banter. No time to even scream for help. The second Katerina said the wizard's name the panther leapt high across the narrow stream, landing with a bloodcurdling snarl at the princess' side.

She barely had time to lift her hands, barely had time to draw in a breath before the thing was upon her. Biting and scratching. Growling and kicking. Lashing out at her bare skin while a heavy paw slashed viciously at the chain around her neck.

Blind instinct took over and she dodged it. Barely.

"Lost this, did you?" she panted, ducking into crouch and rolling to the side. There was a heavy impact as the beast came down right where she'd been standing. "I thought I did, too. But low and behold, it came back to me. Guess it didn't want to get left behind."

A pair of sharp claws swung out of nowhere, raking the side of her face. A warm rush of blood was soon to follow, along with a scream-worthy sting of pain.

If she'd had any sort of blade, it might have been a fair fight. But the gang had lost all their weapons when they'd been ejected from the castle. She was dizzy with wine and hardly clothed, and every step she took was suctioned down in the impossible mud.

No matter. I don't need a blade to have a weapon.

With a fierce cry she lifted her hands, feeling the heat of a thousand flames burning just below the surface of her palms. Her eyes locked upon the giant cat before letting loose a wave of liquid fire, scorching the ground at its feet. It let out a scream and leapt away, shaking out its leg from where the fire had wrapped around its fur. Then it reared up and she was about to fire again, but before she could it vaulted through the air towards her, pushing her down hard upon her back.

Son of a— Of course he has to pick the fastest animal in the jungle!

A shower of sparks exploded from her winded body as she rolled painfully to the side, feeling her ribs splinter and crack under the weight of the jungle cat's massive body. It was just toying with her now. Drawing out the inevitable end. At any point, it could easily bend down and sever her jugular, but it stayed right where it was. Slowly asphyxiating her as she sank into the mud.

"*Help!*" she tried to scream. "*Help!*"

But there was no air behind the words. So there was no sound.

There was another sharp crack and the princess convulsed on the ground, blinded by pain, the frantic pulse of her heart pounding inside her ears. Two more ribs gave way and she knew it was only a matter of time before her entire body shut down. Before this journey of hers ended abruptly, and everything she'd been fighting for was lost forever.

They'd find her body—Dylan and the others. It would take some time for them to realize she was missing, but they would inevitably find this place. And what would they find? After all this time, all the different ways Katerina had imagined her own death, none of them even came close.

The tattered remains of a body? Skin shredded into ribbons? A pale face half sunk into the mud, tangled with bloody braids of crimson hair?

Dylan would never get over it. *Never.* And while the others might eventually find a way to move on, their rebellion certainly wouldn't. Everything they'd been fighting for would be lost.

There was another burst of pain. One that had nothing to do with the panther. A soft sizzle upon her skin. Katerina's eyes opened wide, staring up into the smiling jaws of the beast, but all she could see was her mother's face. All she could feel was the pendant.

Telling her not to give up. Telling her to keep fighting.

With a final burst of strength, she wrenched the amulet from her neck and threw the stone into the panther's yellow eyes. The creature shrieked and leapt away, clawing at its face with a whining screech as the enchanted fire scorched its skin. Finally allowing the princess to push herself up onto her elbows. Finally letting her draw in a shuddering breath.

This is it—last chance.

In what felt like slow motion, she lifted her arms. Her body was weak but the fire was strong, building up in her fingers as she pointed a shaking hand straight at the creature's heart...

...then let out a devastating cry as its razor-sharp teeth sank into her skin.

NO!

The flames vanished, and frantic tears flew down her cheeks as the panther thrashed its head back and forth, taking her hand along with it. Skin tore. Bones snapped. It was a miracle the thing didn't fall off entirely After only a few seconds, there was hardly anything left. Just a mess of blood and the tattered remains of what used to be the princess' hand.

Too breathless to scream, she collapsed upon the ground when it released her. Curling her body in on itself. Eyes and mouth wide open. Shaking with silent sobs.

A looming shadow fell over her, and she turned her face into the mud. It may have been her last moment, but she didn't want to see it coming. Not from him. Not like this. A final convulsion rocked her body and she squinted her eyes shut. Thinking of Dylan. Thinking of home.

SPLASH!

A wave of cold water rushed over her and Katerina's eyelids fluttered open. Lying prone on her side. Staring up in a daze. Unable to make sense of anything she saw around her.

Something was fighting the panther off, but she couldn't tell what. It was moving too fast to maintain any sort of shape. Wisping through the air like the smoky afterthought of a shadow. The sounds were real enough, and they frightened her. Blistering snarls, piercing yips, and a growl so fierce and terrible she knew it would forever haunt her dreams.

They had tumbled into the water. One appeared to be trying to hold the other down. Then a spray of blood shot into the air and they were back on the shore. Flying back and forth with such incredible speed, the princess' eyes couldn't keep up. She could, however, see their tracks.

One set was made by an animal. The other was made by a man.

How is that possible?

Before her mind could properly frame the question, the air around her exploded with one final, tortured cry. A spray of blood splattered the mystical tree, silencing the voices and shimmering bright red against the silver. The air around them seemed to blur, and the next thing Katerina knew the panther vanished with a deafening bang. A bloody raven sprang up in its place.

A raven that screamed in defiance before taking off into the air, heading back to the castle.

...leaving the silhouette of a man in its wake.

He stood there for a minute with his back turned. Silently panting. Hands shaking. Staring up into the sky. Then, with what looked like more than a little effort, he turned to the princess.

"Aidan?"

She only had time to gasp his name before she was up in his arms. Lifted gently out of the mud. Leaving the pools of brackish water behind her. A strangled cry choked out of her throat as he leapt swiftly into the boat, preparing to push it off and take them back to the village.

"My hand," she whimpered, staring down at what little remained. "M-my hand..."

His face went pale when he saw it. Every shred of color vanishing at once. Three times, his eyes flashed between her and the village as a deep uncertainty froze him where he stood. Then, with sudden determination, he lifted her back out of the canoe and lay her gently upon the shore.

"There's no time," he murmured, almost to himself. "I don't want... but there's no time. Not if you want to save your hand..."

She didn't understand what he was saying. The words themselves were getting harder and harder to hear. A wave of dizziness swept over her from head to toe and she let out another quiet whimper, reaching weakly for his hand.

"Don't leave..." she breathed as the world began to fade. "Don't leave me..."

"I'm not going to leave you," he said firmly, squeezing her fingers as tightly as he dared. "And you're not going anywhere. You're going to be fine, Kat. I swear it."

Silly vampire. I'm dying. We both know that.

In a dreamlike sort of trance, the princess slumped back against the ground. Feeling the cool puddles of blood stain the skin between her shoulder blades. Listening as the hum of ancient voices swelled around her like the tide. Watching as Aidan raised his wrist to his mouth and deftly bit open a vein, lowering it down to her level as his other hand looped gently behind her neck.

"Drink," he urged softly, lifting her up. "Drink, Kat. It will heal you."

She registered that he was speaking, but what he said didn't make any sense.

Drink? Drink what? There's nothing here to drink.

"My blood, honey." He read her thoughts, kneeling delicately behind her as he tilted her back against his chest. "Drink my blood. Hurry, before it's too late."

With the utmost care, he lifted his wrist to her lips. The skin was torn, expertly ripped open with a single bite. A thin stream of blood dripped down into her mouth, but she turned her face instinctively away—eighteen years of experience telling her not to.

"Katerina, *please.*" With gentle fingers, he pried her mouth open. Pressing the wound against her lips. "I'm sorry—you have no idea how sorry—but it's the only way. You'll die otherwise."

She coughed and spluttered as the first of the blood dripped down her throat. The taste was familiar, yet foreign. A sharp metallic flavor that repelled her and felt just *wrong.*

Then all at once... it didn't.

A sudden feeling of sensation pricked back into her toes and her eyes opened wider. That sensation started spreading up her legs, and her lips closed around his skin. The blood didn't taste metallic anymore, it tasted sweet. Sweet, and cloying, and delicious. Like a drowning man pulling in a gasp of life-saving air. How could it have ever repelled her? It was a craving that would never fade.

She felt the tug of it flowing through his veins and drank deeper, sinking her own teeth into the edges of the wound. He stiffened but didn't pull away. Letting her take what she needed. Eyes dilating reflexively as he buried his face in his arm.

It was incredible. It was a magic she would have never believed. But it worked.

Little by little, inch by inch, the blood restored her.

From her legs it moved up to her stomach, then to her chest. Stitching together the skin that had been torn open. Supernaturally mending the cracked bones. From her chest it laced up through her neck, healing the clawed gashes and clearing her head, spreading like a wave of pure euphoria down through her arms.

Even in her bloodlust haze, the princess had the sense to pry her eyes open. To gaze in absolute wonder as the bloodied mess of sinew and bone turned slowly back into her hand. Leaving not a single mark as evidence that anything had happened. Not a single scar to be left behind.

It was a sight she would never forget. It was also Aidan's breaking point.

"Okay." He pulled gently on his arm. "That's enough."

A part of her wanted to listen, to honor his wishes, but a far stronger part would never allow such a thing to happen. Her fingers grabbed the back of his hand and fastened on with a strength that surprised her, and she continued greedily swallowing as much as she could.

"That's enough, Kat."

There was a slight strain to his voice as he tried again to free himself. This time she wrapped both arms around his, sinking her teeth even deeper into his skin.

"I said ENOUGH!"

There was a sudden rush of air then the princess slammed into the silver tree, blinking in surprise before sliding back to the ground. She landed on her hands and knees, sinking a moment in the mud before slowly getting to her feet. Staring at Aidan in shock.

Neither knew what to say. Neither knew what to do.

Then the princess said the only thing that popped into her mind. "You threw me into a tree?"

Aidan's normally pale skin was flushed with color. His eyes dilated and overly bright. They fixed upon hers with a completely indecipherable expression as his body went perfectly still. "Sorry. Reflex."

She nodded mutely and dropped her eyes to the ground. They both stood there for a long time, breathing quickly and thinking hard before she lifted her head once more. "You also saved my life."

There was a hitch in his breathing. An involuntary twitch in his hand. "...that was a bit more intentional."

Again, they lapsed into silence.

The princess' head was spinning. There was so much she wanted to ask, so much she wanted to say. But it wasn't as simple as all that. She couldn't tell you exactly how, she couldn't tell you exactly what it meant—but a line had been crossed. And she wasn't sure there was any going back.

"How did you even know where to find me?" she finally asked, breaking the endless silence in a soft, curious voice.

His head jerked up in surprise. He'd been staring at the blood splashed against the tree. "What?"

"You found me," she said again, staring at him with wide, wondering eyes. "None of the rest of them did, not even Dylan..."

It didn't seem possible. If there had been a way to hear the fight from the village, then Dylan would have heard it. He would have shifted, tracked her, and fought the panther off himself. Cassiel would have been right behind him. Along with any other shifter from the camp.

But only Aidan had come.

The vampire hesitated, then bowed his head. "I didn't hear you, if that's what you were wondering. I...I sensed that something was wrong. That you were in trouble. That you were hurt."

A sudden stillness came over Katerina as she stared at him breathlessly. "How is that possible?"

For the second time, Aidan hesitated. His eyes drifted once or twice to the canoe, like he was hoping they could just go back to the village, then he gave up with a little sigh. "It's possible because I've tasted your blood.

The princess' mouth fell open as her eyebrows shot up into her hair. Her first thought was to unequivocally deny it. It was impossible! He never drank her blood, she would have known! Her second thought was to punch the man who'd just saved her life in the stomach. If he had tried her blood, and it certainly seemed as if that was true, she certainly hadn't given her consent.

In the end, she went with option two.

"*Damnit*, Aiden! Seriously?!"

She stepped back with an unapologetic glare, folding her arms across her chest. "You *tasted* my *blood*?" she quoted furiously.

The vampire met her glare for glare "When you *sneezed* it into my *face*!"

The princess took an abrupt step back, then froze in surprise. She remembered like it was yesterday. The way the gang had been attacked by royal guards whilst trying to contact Alwyn. The way Aidan had carried her away from the grisly fight at Dylan's request. The way he'd set her down in the trees miles away from the battle, staring at her in concern and asking if she was all right.

The way she'd sneezed a mouthful of blood right into his handsome face.

"You mean..." she trailed off, staring at him in astonishment. "That...that's all it took?" He nodded, and her astonishment tripled. "Why didn't you say anything?"

He flushed defensively, raking his fingers through his long dark hair. "Well, the lot of you weren't exactly inclined to trust me as it was. Your friends had tried to kill me just a night before, so you'll forgive me for not volunteering it right away."

"But since then," she took a step back towards him, "there's been plenty of time to tell me since then. Why didn't you ever say anything?"

He stared down at her for a moment before dropping his shoulders with another sigh. "I didn't see the point. There was nothing to be done, and it was harmless. I could tell when you were happy, or frightened, or hurt. I could keep track of you, find you if I wanted. But none of that mattered because the connection didn't go both ways—"

He cut himself off suddenly, and the princess understood what was troubling him for the first time. Understood the reason behind that guarded, worried expression.

"...until tonight."

Their eyes met.

"Yeah," he breathed, "until tonight."

Katerina didn't know much about vampires. Only what she'd seen with her own eyes, only what she'd been told. And while a lot of the facts seemed to contradict one another, what she'd learned about the blood connection appeared to be sound.

It was intimate. It was powerful. And it could never be undone.

The princess was quiet for a moment. She didn't know exactly what the ramifications of such a connection might be, but she certainly couldn't regret them now. She couldn't let him either.

"Aidan, you saved my life—"

"I didn't give you a choice," he interrupted heatedly. "Katerina, to force you to drink my blood? It's...it's unthinkable. I never would have done it—"

"You *saved* my *life*." She closed the distance between them, forcing him to look her in the eyes. "You didn't have a choice. And for the record, I most definitely would have chosen exactly what you did. You did what you had to do in order to save me, and it was incredibly selfless and brave. How could you possibly think I'd be angry about something like that?"

His eyes flickered to the village as a strange look shadowed across his face. "I'm not sure everyone is going to feel the same way.

Katerina took a deep breath and slipped her hand into his. His skin was warm, when it was usually cold. Odd—considering she'd taken at least half his blood. Her gaze followed his, and for a moment they just stood there. Both were thinking about Dylan. Both refused to say his name.

To be honest, there was no way to predict his reaction to something like this, but about one thing Katerina was absolutely certain.

"He wouldn't rather see me dead."

The vampire looked down at her for a long moment, then finally nodded. A second later, he glanced back with a shudder at the blood pooled on the ground. "That was Alwyn, wasn't it?"

For the first time, Katerina suddenly remembered that they had recently fought a panther. And while one of them had been magically healed, the other was still sporting the wounds.

"Yeah, it was." She bent down quickly and picked up the fallen pendant, looping it back around her neck. "He was after this."

Aidan stared a moment at the stone then lifted his gaze to the princess, a question in his lovely eyes. "Why does he care? What's so special about it?"

She flashed a quick smile as the two of them headed slowly back to the village. "You know, it's funny you should ask..."

Chapter 9

THE TRIP BACK TO THE village took a lot longer that it probably should have. One of the reasons was that Aidan had been recently mauled by a giant jungle cat. The other was that Katerina wasn't feeling... quite like herself.

"It is SO BEAUTIFUL out tonight!" she exclaimed, lifting her eyes to the stars as her long-suffering companion walked alongside her. When he didn't say anything, she shoved him with an unintentional burst of force. "Aidan, don't you think it's beautiful?!"

He winced as she made contact with his recently dislocated arm, then stuffed his hands into his pockets with a sigh. "Yeah. It's beautiful."

"All the colors here are so bright. I never noticed before." She stood up on her tiptoes, floating rather than walking as they made their way through the trees. "Look! You can see every drop of dew on that little flower. Look how it clings to the bottom of the petals!"

"A perfect night to almost bleed out in a swamp."

She threw back her head, a burst of delighted giggles prompting the first reluctant grin from her vampire counterpart. Her hair was still caked in blood and greenish slime from the bog but she swung the braids cheerfully back and forth, relishing the soft swish against her back.

"I know we're on a strict 'saving-the-world' schedule," she continued brightly, "but I really think we should try to incorporate night hikes into our daily routine. There's just so much to see and do out here; there's no excuse for letting it all pass us by."

Aidan pursed his lips, keeping his eyes locked on the distant lights of the village. "That's a great idea, Kat. You should definitely bring it up at the next meeting."

She flashed him a beaming smile. "I think I will!"

The two walked in silence for several more minutes, winding their way slowly along the starlit path. They would have taken the boat directly back to the center of the village but there was only room for one, and after Katerina got the idea in her head that she wanted to go swimming, Aidan had made the unilateral decision that they should both stick to dry land.

"So, is this how you feel all the time?" Katerina asked suddenly. Her arms were outstretched for balance as she tried her best to walk in a straight line. "Because of your blood?"

Aidan shot her a quick glance, then turned back to the trees. "Is that how I *look* all the time?"

"I'm serious!" She dropped her arms with a giggle, punching him obliviously in the same wretched shoulder. "This is because of your blood, right? Because it's inside me?"

There was a hesitation in his step. One the princess was too wound up to notice.

"I don't feel it the same way you do; it's just normal for me. But yeah," he continued uncomfortably, "I've heard it can give mortals a kind of rush."

"A rush?" She stopped in her tracks, eyes as wide as saucers, seizing the edge of his sleeve. "Aidan... are you saying that I'm *high*?!"

There was a beat of silence.

"You know, this might actually be cute if it wasn't going to get me lynched the second we get back to the village."

"No. No one could lynch you," she said with sudden seriousness. "Aidan, you're a *great* fighter. I couldn't even see you moving you were so fast!"

"Well, thanks." He eased her gently down the path, amused by her childlike assessment of his deadly skills. "I'm going to treasure that."

"You're also *very* good-looking."

"I'll treasure that, too."

She nodded obliviously, leaning back into his guiding arm.

A vague part of her could sense something was off. A vague part had even correctly guessed that it was in connection to her drinking his blood. But just knowing what was going on didn't change the fact that it was happening. And it certainly did nothing to dampen her enjoyment of the euphoric, dreamlike cloud floating around inside her head.

"I'm sorry for not stopping when you asked me to," she blurted suddenly.

One thought tumbled upon the next with little rhyme or reason. Giving neither she nor Aidan any warning or context as to what might come next.

He took one look at her enormous, dilated eyes and bit back a knowing smile. "No, you're not."

She bit down on her lip. "The thing is... I really didn't want to."

He snorted, revealing the hint of a dimple at the corner of his mouth. "At least you're honest."

"In fact..." She eyed him speculatively, the way one might look at the last apple pastry left upon the tray. "I'd actually like a bit more—"

"Hands to yourself." He swatted her slender arm out of the air as it reached covertly for his wrist. "I need to keep a little for myself, you know."

"That's right!" With a belated gasp she stopped suddenly in her tracks, staring at him as if the whole world was coming to an end. "Aidan, you're still hurt!"

"Finally, she notices..."

"Your arm!" she squealed. "Look at your arm!"

"That's right—my arm." He massaged gently at the tendon, unable to keep from smiling at the look of absolute horror on her face. "You want to stop smacking it every ten seconds?"

But the princess had another idea in mind. "Here," she offered as she swept her hair quickly to one side of her neck, "have some of mine."

The smile melted right off his face as his body froze perfectly still. For a second his eyes actually flicked down to the offered vein, then he took a quick step back.

"What—no." He gave her a rough shove forward, gesturing to the path. "Let's go, Kat."

She stayed stubbornly in place, head still tilted as she stared up at him with demanding eyes. "Don't be ridiculous," she insisted. "We already have this blood connection, right? It's not like we can get it twice. You gave me some of yours to heal me. Take some of mine—"

"Stop talking." He looked like he was about ready to drag her back to the village by force but was incredibly hesitant to touch her. He was hesitant even to get close. "Let's just *go*."

"What's the matter with you?" She dropped her hair but refused to budge. Latching onto his guarded expression with the fervor of someone who no longer had any cautious voice in their head telling them to pull back. "You're bleeding like crazy, Aidan. Why on earth wouldn't you?"

"It's not... you wouldn't get it, Katerina." His eyes flashed with frustration. "There are circumstances under which I would drink your blood, and now is not one of them."

"What—a *panther attack* doesn't qualify?!" He shot her a look but said nothing. In the end, she just threw up her hands. "Fine, under what circumstances would you *deign* to drink my blood?"

"If we were together. Screwing."

That shut her up.

Her eyes shot open as her mouth snapped shut. The silence rang out between them, and she lasted only a few seconds under his piercing gaze before she nodded meekly, and the two of them continued walking once more. It wasn't until they reached the outskirts of the village that she shot him a sideways look, staring up out of the corner of her eye.

"I'd prefer you to say, if we were *making love...*"

THE PARTY WAS STILL in full-swing when they got back to the village. In a way, it was almost comical. Just a mile or so down the river, two people had been caught in a bitter struggle for their very lives. But here, people were still dancing and drinking. Completely oblivious to the terror and bloodshed that had raged on within the trees.

Aidan and Katerina cut swiftly through the center of the churning crowd. His hand on her lower back, guiding her with a steady hand. People hardly noticed as they moved past, hardly registered the shredded clothing, the blood and gore until they were already past. At that point the whiskey convinced them they'd imagined it, and they returned to the party with a carefree smile.

All that changed when they got back to the main table.

Cassiel and Serafina were gone—assumedly turned in for an earlier night after passive-aggressively fighting all through dinner—but Dylan and Tanya were still there. They were several bottles of whiskey in. Angled towards each other and laughing at some random story, their faces bright and beaming in the light of the roaring fire.

The princess loved it. She was still firmly under the influence of the vampire's blood, and to see two of her best friends enjoying themselves? So happy and relaxed? Glowing with a gorgeous halo under the light of the moon? She couldn't wait to be a part of it!

"Hey, guys!" She popped up right alongside them, grinning ear to ear. "You miss me?"

The table fell forward as Dylan pushed up from his chair, spilling the entire contents upon the ground. His eyes widened in horror as they swept over her body, lingered in confusion a second on her beaming face, then flickered across the wreckage to where Aidan stood by the fire.

"*What the hell happened?*" he demanded, shouting at the vampire while gathering the princess up in his arms. Tanya pushed to her feet, hands cupped over her mouth, but Dylan was a flurry of movement. Running his hands along Katerina's shoulders. Tilting her head to study the strange dilation of her eyes. Periodically clutching her too hard against his chest, terrified that some mysterious thing had almost snatched her away. "*Speak*, Aidan! What's wrong with her?"

Katerina's brow crinkled into a frown.

Wrong with me? Nothing's wrong with me. I feel fantastic!

"It's all right." The vampire swiftly moved forward, considering his own wounds. "There's nothing wrong—she's fine now, I promise. We were... attacked. In the forest."

"Attacked?!" Katerina could feel Dylan's heart pounding against his ribcage. As hard and pulsing as a drum. She pressed her ear against it with a grin, feeling the vibrations. "By who?"

"By *what*?" Tanya corrected in alarm, running her fingers along the giant animalistic tears in the princess' clothing. Her eyes travelled to Aidan only to see more of the same. "Was it a band of shifters? Are there more of them? I can call my grandmother, rally the guards—"

"It wasn't shifters." Aidan sank abruptly into a chair, looking exhausted. The bright flush he'd gotten after giving Katerina his blood had long since vanished, leaving him shaken and pale. "It was Alwyn. He found her when she wandered off on her own."

It was as if Dylan's worst nightmare had suddenly come to life. His lips parted soundlessly as he stared down at Katerina, too shell-shocked to even wonder why she was grinning with her ear pressed against the side of his chest. In the end, it was all he could do to repeat it.

"Alwyn?" His hands touched the princess' filthy hair, holding her as delicately as if she were a doll. "He was *here*?"

"As a panther," Aidan replied, wincing slightly as he thought back. "It's like he said back at the castle—he can't actually leave. At least, not his corporeal form. We fought him off, but he changed into a raven before we could stop him. Took off through the trees."

"*We* didn't do anything." The princess giggled at the thought. "He's being modest." She lifted her eyes to Dylan, completely oblivious to the worry and tension on his face. "The panther was about to kill me. It had already almost gnawed off my entire hand. Then

Aidan swooped in out of nowhere and forced it back. You should have seen him fighting, babe! He's as good as you!"

The vampire flinched imperceptibly, but it wasn't at the babbling comparison. It was at the rest of what the princess had said. He watched bracingly as Dylan's eyes shot down to Katerina's hand, turning it carefully over in his own. First one, then the other. Then he stared at the vampire.

"...you didn't."

Even Tanya had the sense to back away as the vampire lifted his hands. "Dylan, it isn't what you think. She was dying. Actually *dying*. There wasn't time for me to—"

There was a streak of color, then the vampire let out a quiet gasp. Hands raised. Feet rooted where he stood. Freezing perfectly still as the ranger caught him in a tight embrace.

"Thank you."

Katerina could hardly hear Dylan speak, his voice was so quiet. But in her present state, she could almost feel the weight of what he said. That overwhelming, heartfelt sincerity.

"That's twice now, Aidan." He released the vampire gently, taking care of his own gruesome wounds. "I don't even know what to say."

Now they're BEST FRIENDS!

The princess beamed uncontrollably as the two men stepped back, high as a kite and thrilled beyond measure that everyone she loved was finally on the same page. Clapping her hands like a small child, she ignored Tanya's restraining hand and bounced on the tips of her toes.

"Isn't he the best?" she exclaimed, completely beside herself. "And it wouldn't have even been that big a deal if he hadn't already tasted some of mine!"

Dylan's head jerked up as the vampire's eyes closed with a grimace.

Apparently, it's going to be a very long night...

Chapter 10

A VERY DIFFERENT GROUP of people trudged back to the trees than the ones who had left for the party. Tanya led the way, sticking to the bridge this time, and anxiously clearing a path through the drunken people still milling about. Aidan—whose condition had in no way improved—was managing as best he could, but a one-hundred-and-fifty-foot climb into a tree fort wasn't exactly helping his wounds. Neither was the fact that Katerina had 'borrowed' over half of his blood. At one point his perfect balance failed him, and he actually tumbled back down the steps, saved only when a kind passerby caught hold of his coat. Dylan was a neurotic mess. Torn between a profound sense of gratitude to the vampire, a bottomless loathing toward the wizard, and a bemused exasperation to his girlfriend—who was pausing every few seconds in a fresh attempt to name the stars.

Then, of course, there was that little blood connection to explain...

He'd demanded that Aidan confess what had happened on the spot. Finding himself slipping into a vocabulary that included words like 'confess' and 'corporal punishment.' In his opinion, the notion of Katerina simply sneezing blood seemed like a very flimsy defense. Then again, watching her skip happily around the fire, tracing daisies in the sand, he wouldn't exactly put it past her.

It wasn't until Aidan had collapsed where he stood, his strength and adrenaline finally giving way to massive blood loss, that Dylan stopped the interrogation and rushed forward to help.

Again—it seemed he was in the vampire's debt. Again—it seemed he'd judged too harshly.

The four of them had left the party immediately, and after what seemed like an eternity they had finally made it up to the ranger's room.

By now, the princess was starting to come down a little from the blood. Of course, it was slow-going and came in disjointed waves. She grabbed at the pendant around her neck, screamed in belated shock about her hand, then buried her face in Dylan's, sobbing uncontrollably.

He fought hard to restrain a smile, stroking his hand along the back of her hair. "*That's* more the reaction I was expecting..."

He held her quietly for a while, rocking her back and forth while Tanya helped Aidan down onto the bed, propping him up against the headboards.

"So, how bad is it?" she asked nervously. It was hard to judge a vampire's well-being based on the pallor of their skin. They were too eternally pale for all that. "Let me see."

"It's fine," he said quickly, swatting away her anxious hands with a tight smile. "Promise."

"He's lying," Katerina sniffed, finally pulling her face out of Dylan's jacket. "You were wrestling around with a *panther*, Aidan. Stop trying to be brave."

The vampire shot her a cool glare. "You know, it's really hard to take you seriously when you're still wearing half the swamp."

"At least she stopped singing," Tanya muttered under her breath.

"*Enough.*" Dylan held up his hands for quiet as Katerina glanced down at the thick layer of green slime covering her skin. "We need to figure out what we're doing to do about the wizard, but before that happens I want to make sure that everyone's all right."

To make things fair, he started with his girlfriend.

"Kat?"

She saluted him cheerfully, still feeling some lingering effects of the blood. The second he was distracted, she fully intended to braid his hair.

Dylan nodded, glanced suspiciously at her eager hands, and took a discreet step away. "Aidan?"

"I'm *fine*—really." As if to prove his point the vampire shifted himself higher against the headboard, forcing a tight smile. "Just need a little sleep."

No one believed it. Not even for a second. Tanya reached down with an innocent smile then abruptly squeezed his ankle, reveling in his incriminating gasp of pain.

"Men make the worst patients," she said wisely. "That's what my granny always says."

His eyes flashed as he clutched weakly at his leg. "Your granny decorated herself with pieces of a frog."

Tanya shrugged. It was hard to argue with the logic.

"I tried to offer him my blood, but he wouldn't take it." Katerina turned up her nose, a little offended now that she said it aloud. "Seemed highly resistant to the idea."

Dylan, who happened to know a great deal more about vampires than the princess, looked at her indulgently before flashing Aidan a discreet smile. "And thank goodness for that."

"This isn't something you can just sleep off," Tanya chided patiently. "I'll run back down and get you some animal blood from the village."

Dylan shook his head, catching her elbow as she hurried to the door. "Animal blood is enough to sustain, not to heal. He needs the real thing."

"How do you know that?" Aidan asked curiously.

It was clear he would never have said anything himself. He was about two seconds away from blowing them off and simply going back to his own room.

All the men in the group were notoriously loath to show any sort of vulnerability, but in many ways Aidan was the worst. Call it the vampire curse. Spend enough decades living constantly on your guard, and it becomes almost impossible to imagine living any other way.

"See—this is ridiculous." Katerina put her hands on her hips, purposely ignoring the drops of algae and blood that rained down with her every movement. "I'm *right* here. Just take it."

"You two are connected now," Tanya reminded her. "He can't just take your blood."

"No, but he can take mine."

There was a beat of silence, then—

"What?"

"What?"

"*What?*"

The word echoed back three times with varying degrees of shock as Dylan slipped off his jacket and sat calmly down on the bed. Just a few weeks ago, he would have rather set himself on fire than offer his blood to a vampire. But all of that had changed. Coincidentally, it had changed around the time the vampire in question had saved the woman he loved.

"I've never tried your blood, vampire, and I have no intention of changing that. But you saved her *life*." A belated shiver ran through Dylan's shoulders as he lifted his eyes to Katerina, seeing an entire future that had been snatched back from the brink. "In doing so, you saved mine."

It was a profoundly personal thing to say. A far cry from the sarcastic back and forth that had been flying around the room. It screeched things to a halt, rendering everyone silent.

Really? He'd really do that?

Aidan was frozen with astonishment on the bed. In times of danger or uncertainty, vampires tended to go very still. His lips parted as he tried to think of an appropriate response, then he gave up and quickly shook his head. "Don't be absurd. She's my friend, of course I tried to—"

"You fought off a wizard-panther. That goes above and beyond things you do for a friend."

The vampire faltered and flailed, highly unaccustomed to having his actions thrust into the spotlight. "Regardless, you don't—"

"I owe you *everything*," Dylan interrupted, quiet and compelling. His sky-blue eyes locked intently onto the vampire. "Please... let me at least do this."

For a moment, the world seemed to pause. Both men stared at each other. Both silently taking the measure of the other. Then Aidan nodded his head curtly, and time resumed.

Katerina watched with wide eyes as Aidan hitched himself up higher on the bed, and Dylan tossed his coat upon the floor. For a split second, she thought there was a legitimate chance she was either still high or dreaming. Then she remembered a sudden, but crucial, detail.

"Wait a minute!" She threw up her hands. "Doesn't that mean you'll want to..." She trailed off, too embarrassed to finish, but the others caught her drift. Tanya snorted, and Aidan rolled his eyes, while Dylan shook his head with an affectionate smile.

"Not without having made a connection. This is... intimate. Not romantic."

"Unless you want it to be," Tanya inserted, wiggling her eyebrows.

Katerina smothered a nervous giggle and Aidan tilted his head back with a groan. "This whole thing is a bad idea..."

"Nonsense." Dylan rolled up his sleeve briskly, as if healing wounded vampires was something he did every day. "Go crazy. Take whatever you need."

Only an expert would have been able to detect the flicker of hesitation before he held out his arm. Only someone who knew him very well would have seen the flash of instinctual panic.

He played it off to perfection, but as the vampire reached for his wrist he pulled back with an impulse he couldn't control. Their eyes met, and he was unable to hide the nerves.

"You can stop, right?"

Aidan flashed him a wicked grin. "Let's find out..."

It was quick, but effective. Far different than the experience Katerina had back in the woods.

Dylan looked away as the vampire sank his fangs into his skin. His posture was casual, but his muscles were rigid. His breathing was shallow, but irregular. He tensed when Aidan's teeth tore through his skin, but never pulled away. He even made a concerted effort to relax his clenched hand.

As for Aidan, the vampire took no more than was absolutely necessary. His eyes closed ever so briefly as his fingers wrapped around Dylan's wrist, drinking deeply, but the second his wounds began to heal he released him—holding him steady a moment as the ranger tried to find his balance.

"You okay?" he asked routinely, but there was nothing routine about it.

His eyes were bright, and his skin was flushed with blood. A restless sort of energy seemed to charge the air around him. An energy that reminded Katerina very much of Dylan himself.

"Yeah," Dylan replied a little shakily, swaying slightly on the bed. "Fine."

The vampire glanced down with a guilty flush at the tears in the ranger's skin. "I could heal those for you, but that might make things a bit more personal than either of us would like."

Dylan chuckled and pushed off the mattress, looking a little unsteady on his feet. "I think I'll take my chances, but thanks."

Katerina's eyes shot between the two of them, still unable to fully process what she'd just seen. They were both acting as if nothing had happened, but it couldn't be farther from the truth. A subtle change had sprung up between them. A kind of closeness that hadn't existed before.

She realized, with a hidden smile, that it was very much like the bond between Dylan and Cassiel. A silent protectiveness. Affection hidden beneath layers of sarcasm and scowls.

"What about *you*?" Tanya asked pointedly, ignoring Dylan entirely as she turned instead to the vampire. "Did the blood do the trick? Are you healed?"

"Yeah," Aidan nodded swiftly, pushing off the bed, "it was fine."

"*Fine*," Dylan scoffed, casting a grin over his shoulder as he slipped his jacket back over his arms. "Don't act like it wasn't the best you ever had."

Sarcasm and scowls, all right. It's official. The ranger and the vampire have found a way to make peace.

Aidan shook his head with a sigh, casting a long-suffering glance out the window. "I should have just let the panther eat me..."

THE KREO DIDN'T HAVE baths in the traditional sense. Their strange living accommodations didn't allow for it. But what they did have, Katerina would argue was even better.

"Are you sure we're allowed to be in here?" she asked, tiptoeing over the damp stone and speaking in a whispered hush. "It seems... off limits."

"That's what Tanya said." Dylan followed close behind. "It's all ours until morning."

Until morning?

Katerina wasn't sure exactly what that meant, but she was perfectly willing to find out. That is, she was perfectly willing to find out *after* she'd cleaned off the remains of her disastrous night.

Between her fall into the brackish river, her descent into the mud, and a wizard disguised as a panther slowly bleeding her dry—Katerina was a sight to behold. She hadn't really noticed it before, on account of drinking Aidan's blood, but the second the stuff wore off all crap broke loose.

"Holy crap..." She'd slowly brought her hands up to her face, gazing in breathless horror at her own reflection. "Where's Katerina and what the freakin' A is that thing in the mirror?"

The others had laughed sympathetically. Tanya even raised a hand to clap the princess on the shoulder before thinking better of it and dropping it back to her side. Only Dylan remained completely unaffected. He had already bounced back from the minor blood loss and wrapped his arms around her without a second thought, staring down with a twinkling smile.

"What do you say, beast? You up for a little shower?"

That's when Tanya had told them about this place. About the hot springs fountain, hidden within the caves just above the village. Throughout the day it was teeming with activity, but no one ever came there at night. Just to be sure, Tanya had issued a formal ban. Giving its exclusive use to her friends until daybreak. Allowing them a little privacy before having to face a brand-new dawn.

"This is incredible."

The sense of trespassing wore off and Katerina finally dared to speak at a normal volume, staring around in wonder at the shimmering silica cave.

It was like stepping into a jewelry box. If that jewelry box happened to be filled with pools of water and clouds of steam. The curved walls of the cave sparkled and danced with silver mineral deposits, twinkling like tiny diamonds in the thin shafts of light let in by the moon, and the floors had been worn perfectly smooth. At first Katerina was worried she was going to fall, but the blood kept her steady, giving her perfect balance as she walked to the nearest pool.

The water was hot and steamy, bubbling up from some subterranean lava deposit buried deep in the ground. She trailed the tips of her fingers along the foamy surface as her eyes reflected the luminescent turquoise blue. If the rebellion fell apart and she was ever invited to join the Kreo, she would spend all her time here—haunting the bath house. You'd never get her to leave.

"I have a new plan." She tentatively dipped a bare foot into the water, smiling as the clouds of steam travelled up her leg. "You guys go back to the castle and kill Alwyn. I'll stay here. Focusing on all those 'bigger-picture' problems. Guarding the bubbles..."

There was a quiet laugh from somewhere behind her.

"How noble. Exactly the sort of selfless character we want in our new queen."

Katerina nodded thoughtfully, still staring down into the water. "Darn right."

She didn't notice what he was doing behind her. In truth, she had hardly given any thought as to what exactly was going to happen next, until there was a rustle of fabric and Dylan's clothes landed on the floor. *All* of his clothes.

Her lips fell open with a silent gasp as there was a quiet splash from somewhere deep within the clouds of steam. She lifted her head slowly to see Dylan standing in the middle of the pool, the swirls of foaming water lapping gently against his chest.

"You getting in?"

That's a fair question.

Katerina momentarily froze, crouched like a hesitant statue with the tips of her fingers still trailing in the water. She jerked them out automatically, as if it was somehow inappropriate now that he was inside, and quickly straightened to her feet, slipping at the same time.

"Me?"

...nice recovery.

She resisted the strong urge to hit herself in the face.

The corners of his mouth pulled up in a smile, but he stopped his slow advance, watching her carefully through the misty clouds. "...unless you had something else in mind. Knitting, perhaps?"

He had every right to tease her. She didn't know why she was suddenly so nervous.

They had seen each other naked before, but it had always been at the strangest times. Like when he'd just dug his best friend out of an avalanche. Or when she'd just shed her dragon scales and was standing naked in the middle of the woods.

Why can't we just have NORMAL problems like a NORMAL couple?

Yes, he had every right to tease her. But clearly had no intention of doing so.

The second she froze, he took an automatic step back. The amused smile faded into something more serious. Something without judgement, reassuring and calm.

"If this is moving too fast, I can leave—"

He broke off suddenly as her clothes dropped to the floor. His turn to be speechless.

They had seen each other naked many times, but never intentionally. And always with a barrier. Never was he allowed to just... *look.*

He looked now.

Considering how thrown she'd been when she remembered that bathing implied a certain degree of nudity, she supposed she should have been more nervous now. She hadn't planned on disrobing, it just kind of happened. She certainly hadn't planned on just standing there, but now that she was she had no desire to move. Her heart was steady, every ounce of shyness had melted away.

I am yours, and you are mine.

She remembered his words as they fell asleep that night under the stars.

That includes my body. Let him look.

It was a beautiful gesture. As simple as it was sweet. But Dylan had never been one to merely look. And he had no intention of letting her stand out in the cold.

The second he got over his initial shock he started moving again, cutting gracefully through the water until he was standing right in front of her, just a few feet below. She could see the heat rising off his body. See the individual drops of water clinging to the tips of his lashes. The way his skin had flushed with the steam. He didn't merely offer his hand; he got out first, leveling the playing field. Making things fair.

He saw her. Now she saw him.

She did her best not to stare—an attempt at which she failed spectacularly—then accepted his hand with a small smile as he led her back down into the waves.

It was better than she could have imagined. The feeling of instant relief. The recognition that she'd been sore and cold only a fleeting memory as it faded away in a sea of churning foam. The water was scented. She hadn't realized that before. Laced with an oil that smelled like the sweet-smelling blossoms on the jungle trees. She dipped her head below the waves before she could think about it, coming up slowly as the smell of flowers streaked through her hair.

"Here," Dylan's voice was quiet and uneven, "let me..."

As the princess stood in the center of the pool he went quickly to an alcove cut into the stone, returning a moment later with a jar of the oil they used to scent the water. After a quick permissive glance, he poured some into his hand then lifted it slowly to her hair.

Considering how the night started, it was a truly bizarre way to end.

For the second time in the span of only a few hours, the ranger and the princess were pressed up against each other. Skin to skin. Bodies curving into one. Skin to skin.

Only this time, there was nothing remotely sexual about it.

It was tender.

A shy, sweet sort of tender. Full of long silences and lingering stares. Pounding heartbeats and the tentative hands of two people exploring each other for the first time.

Katerina froze perfectly still as he lifted his arms with quiet dedication, unwrapping her long braids, taking his time with each one. When they were loose, spilling freely over her shoulders, he dripped the oil meticulously over each crimson wave. Combing his fingers through the length of every lock, from her head all the way down to her waist.

It was a slow, methodical process. One that seemed to consume him completely. His hands were unbelievable gentle as they worked the scented flowers into her scalp. Massaging away the stains of blood, caressing away the tears. No detail was too small to go unnoticed and not a single hair escaped his attention as he slowly washed his lover clean.

When he was finished, he filled his hands with water and rinsed the oil away, cupping a hand across the princess' forehead to shield her sparkling eyes.

She thought it was finished. That the beautiful display of devotion had come to an end. But the second the bubbles had rinsed away, he picked up the jar and started all over again. No thought as to repetition or time. Taking her right back to the beginning.

This happened four more times.

At the start of the fifth she opened her eyes, tilting up her face up to his. What she saw there surprised her. Mixed along with the tenderness was a sort of belated fear. The look of a man who'd almost lost the only thing he'd ever loved. Who couldn't bring himself to let it go.

"Dylan," she said softly, reaching up to take his wrists, "I think my hair's clean."

His hands never stopped moving, though his mouth curved up in a smile.

"Not quite."

He dripped in some more oil, letting it pour over her scalp. His hands drifted down to her arms, and he kissed the side of her neck. Kissed the top of her shoulder. Kissed the little hollow at the temple of each eye. Capturing every little part of her with a brush of his lips.

Her breath caught in her chest as her eyes fluttered shut. She could feel his pounding heart against her collarbone. Feel every part of his body pressed against every part of hers.

She had never wanted him more, but at the same time she didn't want him to stop. She could have stood there forever, silently counting his kisses.

So, this is what it feels like. To be truly loved.

As many people had claimed to love her over the years, Katerina didn't know if any of it was the real thing. Her mother may have loved her, but she'd died before the princess could learn the feeling. Her father was incapable. Kailas was under a spell. Alwyn was only pretending. And all the others? Those bands of faceless suitors who had lined up to take her hand?

They didn't know her. They couldn't love her. They loved the idea of the crown.

They would never wash my hair...

She opened her eyes with a smile, gazing up at Dylan's face. She wasn't sure he had ever looked more beautiful. Damp hair curling around his neck. Shimmering moonlight sparkling in his hair. His face wiped smooth with a blissful sort of tranquility as he stared into the princess' eyes.

"Now you."

A flash of anxiety shattered that peaceful calm.

"Sorry?"

Katerina giggled, easing the jar of oil from his hands.

"What? Rangers never wash their hair?"

"No, I just..." An uncharacteristic blush spread across his face, turning her fearless king into a nervous teenager. "No one's ever done that for me before."

"And you think I just go around all day with people bathing me?"

He shrugged his shoulders, regaining a bit of that playful twinkle. "Who am I to fathom the life of a princess?"

She laughed and splashed a bit of water in his face. "Who are you indeed..."

As Katerina was quick to find, the intimate process she'd recently fallen in love with didn't work quite so well in the reverse. She managed to fling enough oil that some of it managed to land in his hair, but that was about the extent of her success.

"You're too tall," she murmured, leaning against him as she stood on the tips of her toes.

"Sorry." He bent his knees with a bit of a smile, putting them on the same level. "Is that better?" Before she could answer his arms circled around her back, pulling her up against him as the jar slipped from her soapy hands. "Or maybe like this?"

"Dylan!" she shrieked, searching blindly in the soapy water before the thing sank forever out of sight. "You can't just—"

But it seemed he could.

With a wild laugh he scooped her up into the air, spinning her round and round as waves of water arced in sparkling circles around them. She let out a breathless shriek and held on for dear life. Wrapping her legs around his waist, and her arms around his neck. Burying her face in his wet hair as her body trembled with peals of uncontrollable laughter.

They splashed a great deal of water out of the stone pool, but neither one of them seemed to notice. In fact, they didn't notice much of anything until they stopped spinning and were left staring into each other's eyes.

I love you.

Katerina let her gaze drift down to his lips. They were parted slightly. Panting from their wild dance with silent, shallow breaths. His heart was pounding, she could feel it pressed against the base of his ribs. And despite the darkness, a radiant sort of light was shining in his eyes.

I love you.

She was ready. More ready than she'd ever been. More ready than she'd ever thought she could be, and more certain than she'd been of anything in her life.

"Dylan, I—"

He pressed a finger over her lips, desperate to speak first. "Could we wait?"

She pulled back in surprise. All those warm, lusty feelings vanishing on the spot. "...wait?"

Did I really just hear that right? He doesn't want to do this?

His eyes swept frantically over her face, tightening with a strange sort of panic before falling to the water. Leaving him with an expression that Katerina couldn't begin to understand.

"I want...I want to do this right, with you."

Those eyes ventured tentatively to her face. Gauging her reaction. Seeking forgiveness. Upon finding a blank expression, he started to panic.

"That sounds ridiculous, I know. And trust me, you have no idea how much I want..." He trailed off, forcing himself to switch course. "But I've done this before. A lot. I mean—" he glanced up with panic, "not a *whole* lot. Not some unforgivable amount of times." He shook his head, every word digging him in deeper. "The point is, never once have a felt... when I think about the two of us together, it isn't like..."

Their eyes met, and he simply shut down. Giving it all up to chance.

"I want us to do this right," he said again quietly, lacing his fingers through hers as he stared nervously into her eyes. "Would something like that be possible?"

It was killing her. KILLING her to agree.

But she loved him all the more for saying it.

"Yes," she whispered, kissing the tip of his nose with a smile. "I think something like that would be possible."

His entire body relaxed in a split second of exquisite relief before coming alive again. His eyes lit up as his hands caught the sides of her face, bringing her closer for a long tantalizing kiss.

She gasped, and giggled, and finally managed to pull herself free. "A little counter-productive at this point, wouldn't you agree?"

They shared a quick look before his eyes lit up with a devilish grin. "Oh, princess, you misunderstand me." His fingers trailed along her ribcage before sliding up her thighs. "I said I want to do this right. Eventually. When the time comes. That gives us plenty to do in the meantime..."

His lips pressed against her neck as he carried her out to deeper water, making her spin as a hungry fire started racing in her veins. They kissed once more, deep and wet, before the corner of her mouth twitched up in a secret grin.

He wanted to wait—that was fine. But she wasn't going to make it easy for him.

Her eyes snapped shut as her head tilted back with a soft moan. "Oh, Aidan..."

His lips disappeared. Replaced with a dry scowl.

"That's not funny."

WHEN TANYA HAD OFFERED Katerina and Dylan use of the hot springs until morning, the princess had thought it was a bit excessive. But now, as the sun slowly rose over the tree line, she was finding it absolutely impossible to leave.

"Just a few more minutes," she murmured, nestling deeper into Dylan's chest. By now, it had become almost as familiar as her own. The lines and curves of his muscles. The faint smell of flowers still radiating from his skin. "That's all I want, I promise."

"That's not all I want..." He moved for the first time in hours, leaning down to bite at her ear. Her head jerked up with a gasp, and she was met with a gentle smile. "But this place is going to be filling with people any minute now. We should go. Or at least find some clothes."

Her brow creased with sudden ferocity as she lifted a stern finger. "What did you promise?" she warned threateningly. "What's the new rule?"

He bowed his head with a grin, spilling his dark hair into his eyes. "No clothes, I know. But I didn't think you'd exactly warm to the idea of all the villagers seeing me like this. So many maidens, all gathered together in the steam... who knows if I could fight them all off at once."

He was obviously joking, but Katerina thought it was actually a decent point.

"You're right," she murmured, amending her new mantra on the fly. "No more clothes, but you must always carry a weapon. Just to be safe."

He laughed again, lifting her lightly to her feet. "I saw some robes in the alcove by the oil. We might want to steal a pair of those, unless you want to put on those swamp clothes again."

"Absolutely not," she said swiftly. "Robes it is."

As he went off to get them, she stretched her arms high above her head. Her brain was waking up with each passing second, and quiet sounds began to filter into the peaceful solitude of their cave. Sounds of the Kreo village coming to life. Opening their doors. Making their breakfast.

Probably for the best that we're leaving. If the threat of discovery wasn't enough, there's always a chance that we might starve...

The ranger and the princess might have agreed that certain things were off limits, but they'd found other ways to work up an appetite in those secret hours before dawn.

"Okay, what do you want? The green or the blue?" Dylan walked out of the alcove holding up two towels, still naked as the day he was born. "I, of course, want the blue. But I'm feeling rather magnanimous this morning, and you can have it if you really..."

He trailed off as he found himself standing in front of a woman who was most certainly not the princess. She was eighty years old, three hundred pounds, and staring at Dylan as if she'd never seen a man in her life. Katerina was standing just a few feet behind. Hands clapped over her mouth.

"...want."

It was horribly quiet for a moment, then the woman held out her hand with an impish smile. "I'll take the green one."

Dylan nodded, swallowed hard, then held out the robe with a forced bit of cheer. "Green it is."

TEN MINUTES LATER, Katerina had yet to live it down.

"—and you couldn't have *warned* me?"

It was the same question she'd heard a dozen times as she and Dylan had fled the bath house at top speeds. As it turned out, she'd gotten the blue robe after all. He was forced to make due with a tiny pink towel wrapped around his waist.

"How was I supposed to warn you?" she exclaimed, nodding a dismissive good morning to the crowds of amused people who stopped to watch as they climbed back up the tree. "I'm telling you: one second the place was empty, the next, she was there! It was like magic!"

"Yeah," Dylan pushed past a group of warlocks with a dry glare, purposely tuning it out when they pointed to his towel. "Those eighty-plus years really spoke to her lightning reflexes."

Katerina held up her hands, thoroughly absolving herself of the whole thing.

"I, for one, maintain that you're overreacting. And at any rate, we're already here." She cast a smile over her shoulder as she pushed open his door. "It's not like anyone else is going to see—"

"About time you two showed up."

The couples looked up with a gasp, just as the door slammed shut behind them. Tanya was sitting cross-legged upon the bed. Aidan was leaning against the window. Both turned with identical smirks as the princess and the ranger came inside.

"Have a good night?" Aidan asked innocently. "You know, I've heard that vampire blood can be quite the aphrodisiac."

Tanya cackled wickedly, pushing to her feet with two cups of cider before stopping suddenly in her tracks. "WOW, someone sure liked the shampoo."

Dylan froze where he stood as Katerina discreetly sniffed at her hair.

Okay, so we might have gone a little overboard with the oil...

"We should get Cass and Sera," the ranger said briskly, purposely avoiding the others' eyes as he discreetly looked for his clothes. "Fill them in on everything that—"

"Already here."

The door pushed open again as the two fae slipped inside, in far better moods than they had been the previous evening. Their eyes were bright and animated, their bodies were lithe and refreshed. There was a spring in their step for the first time in days, and Cassiel had finally released his protective death-grip on his sister.

They stopped moving at the same time, sniffing curiously at the air.

"What the heck happened?" Cassiel asked with a frown. "It smells like someone planted a garden in here."

All of them commented on the oil, but none of them said a word about Dylan's towel. Odd that *that* detail was considered normal.

Dylan blushed and muttered something about needing to find new friends, while Katerina sat down with sudden briskness on the bed beside Tanya, eager to get the story out in the open.

"So a lot happened after you two left the party last night," she began quickly. "I wandered off to this talking tree to find answers, discovered some great news about my pendant, and figured out what we need to do to win this war. Then Alwyn attacked me—disguised as a panther—and bit off my hand. Aidan gave me his blood and healed me, forging a mystical connection between the two of us, but he got hurt in the process. So when we got back to the village, which took a little longer than usual because I was high, Dylan gave Aidan some of his blood as well."

There. That sums it up rather nicely.

Brother and sister blinked at the same time. Trying to process. It was quiet for a second before Cassiel turned to his friend in disbelief.

"Wait a minute... you let Aidan drink your blood?"

Serafina rolled her eyes with a half-smile. "And here I was hung up on the talking tree..."

"I'd like to hear a bit more about winning the war—if you don't mind," Tanya interjected, the unexpected voice of reason. "Can we circle back to *that* please?"

"Right—*that*." Katerina tucked her hair behind her ears, staring at each one in turn. "When I went down to this tree, they call it the truth tree, I met up with Tanya's grandmother who told me that my pendant isn't a pendant at all. It's an *amulet*, meant for protection."

Tanya chewed her lip contemplatively. "Are you sure she wasn't drunk?" Aidan shoved her in the back. "What? She drinks a lot..."

"Anyway, that got me thinking. Protection, protection, where had we heard that before? And then it hit me!" The princess slammed her hand against the headboard in triumph, making them all jump. "Alwyn. *Protected through grace as only one can?* Guys, the key to winning the war is the prophecy."

She expected instant approval. She expected them all to light up with the same realization at the same time. What she didn't expect was silence.

A silence that stretched on, and on, and on...

"The prophecy?" Cassiel finally broke it, his voice full of doubt. "That's a bit of a stretch."

"A *stretch*?" Katerina couldn't believe her ears. "Are you kidding me?"

"He's right, Kat," Tanya chimed in reluctantly. "If the key to winning the war was based on some kind of prophecy, then why on earth would Alwyn tell us about it right before?"

"He didn't!"

"He totally did," the shape-shifter insisted. "You just said—"

"Guys, listen to me." Katerina held up her hands, desperate for them to understand. "Alwyn didn't let it slip; he said it because he thought we were all about to die. In his mind, it was the big climactic moment. The one he's been waiting for all these years. And when that didn't work, he turned himself into a freaking cat just to steal back my pendant."

"Amulet," five people corrected her at the same time.

"It's the prophecy," she concluded. "It has to be."

She was starting to sway them. She could tell. It was hesitant at first, but it was the only bit of hope they had left, and before long they found themselves holding on with both hands.

"So what do we do?" Aidan asked directly.

Katerina didn't miss a beat. She'd been waiting for someone to ask. "We talk to the one person who might have any idea what prophecy Alwyn's talking about. The one person who might actually know where the prophecy might be."

She turned to Dylan, her eyes glowing with anticipation. He stared at her curiously for a moment, then his face lightened in surprise.

"Michael?" he asked. "You want to ask Michael?"

She nodded fervently.

"Who else could possibly know? The man has the history of the known universe locked up in that little library of his. Surely he has to know something about this."

The others nodded slowly, latching on to the plan.

"What we need to get is another seeing stone," Tanya murmured, thinking on the fly. "They aren't easy to come by, but I might know a place where—"

She was interrupted by a sudden knock on the door. The group froze, then Dylan remembered it was technically his room and called out, "Who is it?"

"It's Gemma!"

His brow furrowed in confusion, but Tanya rushed forward and pulled open the door. A tiny child stepped into their midst, trembling from head to toe.

"What is it, honey?" Tanya sank to her knees at once in front of her. "What's wrong?"

The girl's eyes widened as she stared at the imposing group standing in front of her, resting a moment on the vampire and the fae. Finally, her eyes came to land on the princess. A tiny shudder rippled through her shoulders, but she forced herself to be strong.

"The hunting party. They found something out in the desert."

It was a second before she qualified her words.

"...they found *someone*."

Chapter 11

KATERINA DIDN'T SAY a word as she marched with the others through the jungle. The rest tried to engage her several times but she kept her mouth in a tight, thin line, her eyes straight ahead and her hand clasped tightly in Dylan's. The report from the hunting party had been vague. Most of them had stayed in the desert to wait for the others. The only reason little Gemma came back with the news was that the little girl apparently shifted into a cheetah and the fastest messenger they had.

They didn't technically know who was waiting for them out there in the scorching sand. And yet, there wasn't a doubt in Katerina's mind. She didn't know why. She didn't know how. She didn't know if it was something she could trust. But there wasn't a doubt in her mind.

"They're right up here," Gemma murmured. Since they'd left the village, she'd yet to let go of Tanya. Cassiel walked right behind them, staring at their hands. "Around the next bend."

To Katerina, the rolling sand all looked the same. Ever since they'd left behind the cover of the trees and were hit with a wall of unbearable heat, she'd had to rely completely upon the instincts of others. But Tanya apparently knew what the girl meant.

She thanked her, gave her hand a squeeze, and sent her back to the village. A moment later she made a sharp turn and the six friends came up to the top of a hill, gazing at the people below.

There you are.

Even from a distance, Katerina would know him anywhere. The tall silhouette. The graceful slope of the shoulders. The wavy hair. Even blurred like a mirage, there was no mistaking the curve of his brow. The sharp set of his jaw. The dark eyes roving over the sand.

It was him, all right.

It was her brother.

"Kailas."

She whispered the name, but the sound seemed to carry all the way down into the dunes. He lifted his head sharply, and for a suspended moment the two of them locked eyes.

She didn't need to be frightened; there was no way he could move. At his back were miles upon miles of sun-parched desert. And in front of him was a crescent moon of Kreo spears. Each one was pointed at his chest. Each person holding one was just waiting for an excuse.

As if that wasn't enough, there were the people standing by her side.

Cassiel had almost murdered the prince once, and after what she'd seen last night there was no limit to what Aidan could do. Then there was Dylan himself. Katerina could honestly say she couldn't imagine a worse enemy to have than her terrifying, beautiful boyfriend.

And yet, the second she saw Kailas it was like her feet refused to move. A childhood fear is a hard thing to shake. Especially when it's calling out your name.

"Katerina!"

His voice was desperate. His body almost unable to stand. He took a compulsive step towards her, then instantly stumbled back as a dozen glinting spears came up to meet him.

"Kailas!"

It wasn't the princess who answered, but the beautiful fae standing by her side. Serafina took one look at the scene in front of her before racing down the hill, escaping even her brother's lightning-fast hand. Cassiel called out something in a foreign tongue, a fierce warning, but his little sister didn't listen. She just went tearing towards the captive in the sand.

In the end, they had no choice but to follow.

Like a flood the six friends raced down the hill, the scorching ground thundering beneath their feet, coming to a sudden stop just behind the line of guards.

It was a guard who had stopped Serafina. Holding her back with strong hands.

"Sera," Kailas gasped, seeing her for the first time. His eyes drifted down to the soldier's restraining hands and flashed with indescribable anger. "*Let her go!*"

It was strange enough to hear, even if he hadn't said it at the exact same time as Cassiel.

The two men looked at each other for a moment before Cassiel strode forward briskly, taking his sister back under his arm. Kailas looked like he wanted to run forward as well, hold her, comfort her, but he held himself back, turning to a sister of his own.

"Katy," he breathed, practically shaking with relief. "I can't believe you're here."

Up close, he was in even worse shape than when they'd left him back in the dungeon.

His face was gaunt and bruised, his hair was matted with blood. There was an unnatural paleness to his skin, and deep circles hollowed beneath his eyes—eyes that were wincing painfully against the light of the sun. He wasn't wearing any clothes, save for a pair of dark pants that hung loosely on his hips, and the sight of his body was enough to make his sister gasp aloud.

"Hasn't he been feeding you?"

The words were out of her mouth before she could stop them, hanging like a dark cloud in the air. There might have been a way to fake a spell, but it wasn't possible to fake months of near-starvation. Her brother, so fit and strong, had withered away. His legs were weak and trembling. A near-constant tremor shook his hands. Still—the sight of her made him smile.

It wasn't Kailas who answered, but Serafina.

"They gave us food for one," she said quietly. "We'd been splitting it."

A sudden surge of anger rocked Katerina's body, and Cassiel made a dangerous sound under his breath. She pictured the two of them the last night at dinner. The way Serafina had been completely unable to eat. Her body decimated by months upon months of hunger.

"That doesn't matter now." Kailas squared his shoulders and took a step, reaching tentatively for his sister's hand. "Katy, I—"

Dylan was nothing more than a blur. One second, he was standing by Katerina's side. The next, he'd taken a sword from the nearest guard and was holding it to her brother's throat.

"How did you escape?" He pressed the blade against Kailas' neck, digging it in deep enough to find blood. "How did you get out of the castle?"

The prince's face paled as he slowly lifted his hands into the air. His eyes flashed to Katerina but she stayed where she was, needing to hear the answer for herself.

"I would never hurt her," he said softly, eyes shining. "You have to know, I would *never*—"

"I'm not going to ask you again." Dylan shifted forward so that Katerina was blocked from view. "How did you escape the castle?"

For the second time, the prince blanched. For a second he actually glanced behind him, as if he might find answers buried in the sand. Then he stared at the ranger, shaken and lost.

"I just..." He trailed off and started again. "Back in the cell, Alwyn... he told me things I didn't remember. Things he'd made me do." A shudder rocked his entire body, shaking him where he stood. "I didn't know how it happened, I was just so angry..."

The blade dug in deeper, and a look of genuine fear shot across his face.

"...you won't believe me."

But all at once, Katerina did believe him. There was something about his face. Something about those particular words. About what she knew she and her brother were capable of when triggered with the proper emotion.

I was just so angry...

"You shifted into a dragon."

A gasp went through the guards as her brother went suddenly still. His eyes widened as they locked on his twin, and for a moment there was no one in the world but the two of them.

"Yes." It was barely a whisper, like a brush across the sand. "How did..." Their eyes met, and his mouth fell open with a gasp of his own. "...*you?*"

"Quite the family secret, huh?" She walked through the line of guards, ignoring the row of spears, ignoring the hissed words of warning. She walked until she was standing right in front of her twin, moving Dylan's blade aside with the tip of her finger. "Congratulations, brother. It looks like you finally got the power that Alwyn always wanted."

For a second, they simply stared at each other. Then a look of horror flashed across his face.

"Katy, I'm so sorry."

He truly did look it. He looked like he would have given the rest of his life to erase what had happened. The others tensed automatically, the guards gripped nervously at their spears, but somehow Katerina knew exactly what her brother was going to say.

"...he took it from me."

THEY NEVER MADE IT back to the village. They only got halfway there before tensions boiled over and the entire hunting party dissolved into a vicious argument. The guards versus the friends. The guards versus the guards. The friends versus each other. There was no end in sight.

No one could decide the best course of action. No one could decide what to do.

And, of course, everyone thought *they* were right.

As fate would have it, only two people didn't get involved. They sat together—close, but not too close—on a stone ledge alongside the path. Silently watching. Occasionally sighing. Finally, when she could no longer stop herself, Katerina cast a sideways glance at her brother.

"Where did you find pants?" she asked him quietly.

He glanced down, swinging his legs gently against the stone ledge. "Stole them. One of the guards back at the castle, before Alwyn exiled me." He shot her a quick look, then rolled his eyes. "I know, you don't approve."

She stifled a grin, her mind racing back through all the laws she'd broken since her own exile. "You'd be surprised..."

He turned his head with a faint smile and their eyes met. They stared for a long moment, taking in all the things they'd missed, then that smile slowly faded from his face. "Katy... about these last few months. About our *father*. I don't even—"

"Let's not talk about that now," she interrupted, holding up a bracing hand. "Let's just focus on getting from one day to the next, all right?"

He nodded quickly and let the conversation drop.

There was too much to say. Too much to say, so why bother starting. The past was a mess and it seemed like the only thing they could do was try to move forward.

Granted, that was easier said than done.

"So," Kailas tried to get the ball rolling, gesturing with a forced smile to the escalating confrontation raging on in front of them. A confrontation that centered mostly around 'what do to with the dangerous prince. "These are your new friends?"

Katerina betrayed not an ounce of emotion. "Well, you killed all my old friends, so..."

The prince blanched and lowered his eyes to the wall. For a moment, he simply sat there, scrambling for something to say, before he finally raised his head with a mild. "They seem nice."

Nice?

The princess actually shot him an incredulous smile.

At the moment, Dylan was violently arguing with what looked to be the commander of the guards, Aidan was standing behind him, fangs bared, Cassiel had pulled out an actual blade and was threatening decapitation, whilst Tanya was shifting into different people at the drop of a hat, whoever seemed to be bothering her the most. The only one staying out of the fray was Serafina, and even she was twirling a dagger between her fingers, staring at the man who'd restrained her.

Sure. Nice.

Kailas caught her staring and laughed softly under his breath. "Fine. They look like a band of vicious cutthroats. What do you want me to say?"

Katerina knew he was teasing. She even knew she'd left him no other option. But the second he tried to move forward, her own humor faded completely away. Her eyes flashed with eight years of pent-up anger before gesturing back to the group.

"That band of 'vicious cutthroats' kept me alive when my own brother put a bounty on my head. So, what do I want you to say?" Their eyes locked. "I want you to say thank you."

His face tightened painfully, and he pulled in a deep breath. Overwhelmed to the point of breaking. Stricken to the point of simply wanting to give up. But no version of Kailas was the kind to give up. No matter how culpable he might be. No matter how long the road to redemption.

"And I will," he said softly, keeping his eyes on the ground. "I'll say it as many times as they can stand to listen."

For what felt like the hundredth time that day, Katerina tried not to act as surprised as she felt. It would be one thing if her brother had been perfectly normal growing up, and only in the months since her father's death had suddenly fallen under a personality-changing spell. It would be different if she was used to this softer side of him. The side that wanted to do good.

But that just wasn't the case.

Alwyn's darkness worked slowly. Twisting and manipulating. Making subtle changes, until you couldn't find your way back to the place where you started. For almost half of her life, Kailas had been the monster she knew him as today. So many years that she didn't know what part was the spell and what part was her brother. So many years, she abruptly realized she didn't know her brother at all.

"I know you can never forgive me," he said suddenly. "I know I can never start to make this right. The things he made me say, the things he made me do..." He broke off with a shudder—her brother who *never* shuddered. Bowing his head. Catching his breath. A broken man. Nothing like the arrogant adolescent the princess had left behind.

Maybe this is the real him.

The thought overwhelmed her, and she felt the sudden urge to hold him. To feed him. To protect him from whatever was going to come. Just like when they were children.

Her lips parted as she reached out a tentative hand, but before Kailas even saw what she was doing a sudden word caught his attention and his head snapped up.

"Retreat?" He slid off the ledge, landing painfully on his feet. "Now is the worst time to retreat. Now is when we need to strike."

The entire forest fell silent as both sides of the argument slowly turned around—their eyes burning a hole in the renegade prince. He looked very much alone. One man standing against all the rest. Before Katerina knew what she was doing, she hopped off the ledge and stood beside him.

"Why would you say that?" she asked quietly.

"Why would you think it was all right for you to speak at all?" Cassiel interjected sharply. His sister flashed him a furious look, but the fae didn't care. One hand was still gripping his knife.

Kailas hesitated. He clearly hadn't been planning to speak, and he didn't seem eager to speak against Serafina's brother—whatever the cost. But some truths were too powerful to ignore. "Alwyn might have my power, but it doesn't belong to him. It doesn't respond to his command. It's unpredictable; he can't control it." His eyes flickered around the humid trees. "That's how we all ended up here. He'd meant to kill us, not send us away."

Tanya shifted cautiously, her eyes locked on the prince. "Well, if any of that's true, it's good news. But it doesn't change anything—"

"It changes *everything*," Kailas interrupted passionately. "Every day we wait to attack is another day Alwyn has to learn to control the power. If we wait too long, he'll master it. And once he does, I don't know if there's anything we can to do stop him."

"And that's what you want?" Dylan slowly walked forward. His piercing eyes locked on the prisoner. His voice dangerously quiet. "You want to *stop* him? To what end?"

The final question, he didn't ask. But somehow it was asked anyway. An accusation as clear as a threat. Ringing out in the silence that follow.

So you can take your sister's throne?

It was like he'd thrust a knife straight into Kailas' chest. The prince stiffened suddenly, drawing in a sharp breath. His eyes flashed as eight years of dark magic warred their way through his system. Battling a future that might have been. Battling the man left behind.

After a few seconds, he finally spoke.

"The crown isn't mine." His voice was just as soft as Dylan's. "Katerina is the older twin; the throne is hers by right. I would do nothing to challenge that." He took another deep breath. "When this is all over, I can do whatever you want. Go far away. You never have to see me again. But none of that can ever happen if Alwyn figures out how to harness the magic first."

The rest of them stared at him for a long time. Each coming to their own conclusions. Each rendering their own silent judgement. When enough time had passed Dylan finally turned to Katerina, leaving the decision entirely in her hands.

"What do you think?"

She paused. Looked at her brother. Then made her up mind.

"I think we need to act fast."

Chapter 12

FOR THE REST OF KATERINA'S life, no matter how long that might be, she knew she would never forget what happened next. The people who were with her. The things she'd seen.

It started completely by accident. An unexpected escalation of her plan.

"—need to assemble the others," she was saying, head bent close to Dylan's as they hurried along the forest path, talking strategy. "*All* the others. Not just Belaria's army. That means calling in favors from the people at Vale. Sending a message to Petra to gather the rebel camps and meet us somewhere near the castle. If we hurry, we can probably make it before—"

"*Kat.*"

Dylan pulled up short, stopping them in their tracks. Katerina took one look at his shocked face before following his gaze. A second later, she was stunned into silence herself.

They were all there. Everyone she'd been talking about. Everyone they'd been planning to assemble. They were all standing in the center of the village. Gazing back at her with steady smiles.

"How is this possible?"

Katerina's eyes widened in astonishment as they swept over the group.

Belaria's army alone was massive, swelling the confines of the village to their very peak, but Katerina saw familiar faces as well. People from places she never thought she'd see again.

There was a coven of witches the gang had met back at the festival of woodland lights, the same women who'd thrown Katerina out of their tent for having red hair. Mika, the succubus bartender, was standing amidst a group of shifters from one of the taverns they'd stopped at along the way. She caught the princess' eye and gave her a wink. A group of vampires was standing a little way off by themselves—vampires Katerina didn't know, but who nodded in solidarity at Aidan. A trio of nymphs they'd threatened while posing as officers of the law. The same ghastly hag who'd tried to purchase one of her eyes. There was a frantic waving from beside one of the trees, and Katerina looked up in shock to see Bernie the giant grinning from ear to ear—unaware that the people around him had scattered to avoid getting trampled by his bouncing, excited feet.

It was a congregation of all those people she'd met along her journey. All those different faces who'd helped shape her opinions and guide her path.

Petra was standing in the front of the group. Along with Tanya's grandmother, Henry Chambers—the magistrate of Vale, and the acting-commander of Dylan's own army. Atticus Gail.

They stepped forward at the same time, a coordinated greeting. But before they could say a word, they were waylaid by a sudden barrage of blinding lights. Yellow, gold, and purple. Before the princess' eyes could even adjust she began to hear tiny voices coming out of them. Voices that grew in volume as the lights themselves grew in size.

"—lucky we made it here at all! If we'd listened to you—"

"—for the hundredth time, Beck, I said I was sorry! How was I supposed to know we had to turn left when we got to the falls—"

"Would the two of you just shut up?! Look! We're here!"

There was a little *pop* as the lights disappeared, leaving three tiny women standing in their place. Women with bright dresses, even brighter hair, and a trio of radiant, supernatural smiles.

I don't believe it!

"Marigold!" Katerina rushed forward with a gasp, sinking to her knees at once to give the fairy a proper hug. "What are you doing here?"

The woman beamed back at her, rosy cheeks and golden curls. "Well, we couldn't very well miss this, could we? We've been keeping track of your adventures, ever since we sent you off in search of *this* one." She flashed Dylan a motherly smile. "Nice to see you again, kid."

Kid?

He stepped forward as well, dropping to his knees in order to give the fairy a quick kiss on the cheek. "It's good to see you. I thought these two might have driven you to an early grave."

The dark-haired fairy standing beside them stuck out her tongue, while the other flashed an impish smile. Neither one denied it for a single second.

"We *dated*, you know," Nixie whispered loudly to Katerina.

Dylan pushed to his feet, shaking his head with an exasperated smile. "I told you... that wasn't dating. It was stalking. And I was fourteen."

"Semantics."

"Give the children some air," a deep voice interrupted. "It looks like they've already had a long day. And heaven knows, it's not over yet."

Katerina jumped at once to her feet, stunned silent by the greatest surprise of all.

Michael.

And not just Michael. It looked as though half of Talsing Sanctuary had taken up the cause.

The crowd parted automatically to let the man through, gazing appreciatively at the small army he'd brought with him. They were armed with bows and spears—an impressive collection, though Katerina had no idea what it was doing in a pacifist's monastery. She recognized Randall, the shifter who'd given them so much trouble, standing in the middle. For the first time, there was no hint of antagonism when they locked eyes. He simply nodded his head with a little bow.

"*Michael.*" Dylan stepped forward in surprise, staring at the man who'd saved his life and basically raised him. "What are—"

"This fight concerns our future," Michael interrupted lightly, his twinkling eyes resting with great affection on the ranger's face. "That means it belongs to all of us. From the humble soldier, all the way up to the king."

Their eyes met, and a knowing look passed between them.

The man might have been as isolated as could be, but he knew exactly what had happened in Belaria. He knew exactly the step Dylan had taken, and what it would come to mean.

"On that note, I thought you could use a few more soldiers..."

He gestured to the horde behind him, all of them chomping at the bit, before coming to take his place among the others. A brief handshake was exchanged with Gail and Chambers, but he and Petra came together in a warm embrace.

"Brother," she murmured, smiling into his waves of hair, "it's good of you to come."

Katerina's eyebrows shot up as she exchanged a quick look with Dylan.

Brother?

He looked as baffled as her. Michael meant enough to him that it looked as though he was actually going to ask the question, but a tap on the shoulder made him turn around.

"We made ready as soon as we got your message." Atticus Gail looked him up and down with a casual smile. Casual, but he was anxiously checking his liege lord for any scrapes or damages he might have incurred along the way. "The entire Belarian force is assembled—at your command."

"But how did you know where to go?" Tanya interjected. It didn't matter that the people speaking were kings or princes—the shifter made a habit of assuming all high-level conversations would automatically include her. "We didn't plan on ending up here ourselves."

"Marigold told us," Henry Chambers answered with a smile. "And I must admit, it was the strangest message that's ever made it over the mountains and found its way to Vale."

Katerina snorted under her breath and cast a quick look at the fairies. *I'll bet.* She could only imagine their fantastical alternative to normal post.

"At any rate, we came as promised—but we're still unclear as to the reason." Petra's piercing gaze swept past her brother and onto the princess. "I'm assuming you have a plan."

Suddenly, the eyes of the entire village were upon her. Every waiting soldier. Every creature of magic who had gathered alongside. Even Bernie stopped bouncing long enough to listen.

A tremble of nerves swept over her at the spotlight, but she forced her voice to be strong. "Yes, I do."

Her heart skipped a beat as her eyes zeroed in on one man in particular.

"But first... I have to talk to Michael."

"A PROPHECY?"

Three people were sitting in the chief's hut—Katerina, Michael, and Dylan. She'd wasted no time whatsoever in telling him what had happened back in the castle dungeon. About Alwyn's brutal betrayal, the prince's unfortunate spell, and the one weapon that might help them win it all.

She'd been assuming Michael could help. Between Dylan's confidence in him and what she'd seen for herself, he was one of those infallible people who seemed to know everything and could do no wrong. She hadn't, for a second, thought he wouldn't be able to help them.

But the second she mentioned a prophecy his face went blank.

"I'm sorry, children, but I'm not in possession of such a thing." His eyes were troubled as they gazed out towards the water. "And I'm sorry to hear about Alwyn. I'd always considered him to be a friend."

Katerina remembered when Alwyn had first told them to go to Talsing Sanctuary. That he'd be sending a message on ahead in order to allow them entry. She'd thought at the time that he was just doing it for her protection. Little did she know he was hoping Michael could help her unlock her power, so he could steal it for himself, once and for all.

"But surely you've heard of such a thing," Dylan pressed, unable to accept that his unfailing mentor could suffer such an important lapse. "He took Adelaide Grey's amulet off my neck and said, 'Protected through grace, as only one can...' Surely that means something to you."

Michael leaned back in his chair, looking abruptly thoughtful. "If the amulet is meant to protect and the danger is readily apparent, then the question becomes who is that protection for." His eyes rested upon each of the youngsters in turn. "It's no coincidence—the strange assortment of people who showed up at my door. A queen of men, a king of shifters, a prince of the Fae. I didn't know about your friend Tanya's lineage until we arrived, but between that and the inclusion of a vampire—you represent the five kingdoms of old."

The five kingdoms *of old*?" Katerina repeated, stressing the last bit. "What does that mean?"

"Back in the days when this earth was still young," Michael explained, "it was divided into five separate empires. Each remaining autonomous from the others, while vowing to unite if they ever came under threat. The kingdoms were that of Men, the Fae, Shifters, Vampires, and all those whose blood and background rendered them without clear affiliation—the Kreo. For centuries, the people prospered under a lasting peace. It wasn't until the first Damaris came to sit upon the Throne of Men that the balance shifted, as one kingdom attempted to consolidate the power of the rest."

Typical. Centuries of prosperity, then my family steps up to the plate.

"If I had to guess, I'd say that the heads of those five kingdoms—represented by each of the people you've gathered today—would be the ones for whom such ancient protection would be meant. That if they were to unite, like the days of old, they could stand together against any evil."

Katerina blinked as all but a fifth of her prospective empire went up in smoke. Could she really do it? Could she give up all everything except the High Kingdom—return the lands to their rightful people—all in the name of peace? Could she possibly sacrifice so much?

"Yes."

The word flew out of her mouth before she'd made the decision to say it. Both Michael and Dylan looked at her in surprise, but she had never been more sure of anything in her life.

"Five kingdoms, for five groups of people. United in peace." The amulet glowed warm against her chest as she flashed a quick look at Dylan. "Sounds fair to me."

She had never seen him so proud. His entire face was aglow with it, watching her with silent, beaming eyes. But there was no time to revel. There was no time to do anything at all.

"In that case, the path before us seems clear."

Michael's lips thinned to a hard line as he braced himself for what was to come.

"We go to war."

KATERINA AND KAILAS had grown up in the time of the rebellions. They had lived in the castle when it was under siege, they were accustomed to seeing the royal army marching out to fight. The enemies of the Damaris family were numerous, and it seemed like hardly a season would go by before some particular faction needed to be subdued. It became part of their regular lives. As normal as sitting down for their studies or going riding through the woods.

But they had never once been on the other side.

"This feels very strange," Kailas said softly, standing by Katerina's side as they stared up at the castle through the trees. "Like something out of a dream."

"That's just the after-effects of the portal," Tanya answered obliviously, clapping him with a bit too much force on the back. "You'll get used to it."

The portal had been yet another surprise.

It seemed that Alwyn had unintentionally banished the group to the middle of the desert because it was as far away from the High Kingdom as one could possibly get. When Katerina had discovered the distance, her face had fallen in despair. It would take at least two months for such a large group of people and supplies to get back to the castle. Plenty of time for the wizard to have mastered Kailas' power. What were they supposed to do?

Fortunately, she'd happened to ask the question in a land running with deep magic.

With a wrinkled smile the princess would never forget, Tanya's grandmother—High Priestess of the Kreo—had led the thousands of people assembled out to the very edge of the burning desert. Once they were there she pulled two stones from her pocket, hit them together with a shower of silver sparks, and stepped back as a flaming gateway appeared right in the middle of the sand.

"Good luck," she called as, one by one, they stepped through the magical arch. "I'm afraid you're all going to need it..."

It was a masterful save, but the enchanted doorway clearly wasn't for everyone. The men and the vampires had all required at least an hour to recover. Poor Bernie had stumbled around so dizzily, he collapsed on top of a small grove of redwoods.

"Thanks..." Kailas smiled until the shape-shifter was gone, moving along down the line, then turned his eyes back to the castle. "But not exactly what I meant."

Unfortunately, Katerina *did* know exactly what he meant. She was feeling the same thing. It might have highly counterintuitive, but something about lying in wait in the woods outside their childhood home, waiting to attack, felt instinctively wrong. How many times had Katerina stood on the stone balcony herself—gazing down at scores of her father's enemies, all doing the same thing?

"You want to go back to the village?" she asked with a hidden smile. "I'm sure there are still a few dozen people there who'd like to tie you to a chair and beat you to death."

It was true. In light of the present situation with the wizard, the issue of the spellbound prince had been temporarily shelved for a different day. But that didn't mean there weren't plenty ideas of what to do with him in the meantime. When it was suggested that he be allowed to come and fight, Dylan himself had thrown such a tantrum Katerina didn't know if he'd ever recover.

Kailas flashed her a wry look, something that reminded her very much of when they'd teased each other back and forth as kids. "You'd like that, wouldn't you? However much it pains me to say, I'm sure my darling sister would be the very first in line."

She shrugged with a little grin. "They say it's unhealthy to bottle up emotions. Best to let things air out."

He snorted and shivered at the same time. "In that case, I'm happy to help."

The breeze picked up as Katerina cast a silent look at her brother. He was already looking stronger—just after having had a decent meal. The color in his face had been washed out by the silver moonlight, but he was no longer swaying on his feet. A hard sort of determination had come over him. Tensing his muscles and glinting like steel in his dark eyes.

"I'm sorry about your power," she said quietly, realizing it for the first time. "I'm sorry he took it away from you. It came from our mother. You should be the one to have it, not him."

To her great surprise the prince shook his head, keeping his gaze locked on the castle.

"I'm not sorry. In fact, I'm happy to be rid of it." He felt her watching and turned to her with a sad smile. "After everything I did... I don't deserve it."

She sucked in a sudden breath, making the decision once and for all. "You were under a spell." Her voice was quiet but firm. Unwavering, despite everything that had happened. "The things that happened weren't your fault. It wasn't *you*, Kailas."

He tore his eyes away from the castle, staring at her in shock. For a second, a desperate kind of hope shone in his eyes before being immediately replaced with an instinctual sort of caution. "Do you really mean that?" he asked quietly, eyes locked onto hers. "Katy, do you think there's a chance that you could ever—"

He broke off as a wave of fire shot across the sky. As blinding as it was terrifying. Lighting up the forest as the princess and her army stared up in from under the trees.

"He did it," Kailas whispered, gazing up in horror. "He figured it out."

For a second, the twins simply stood there. Side by side. Hand in hand. Faces illuminated with flashes of violent color as they stared up at the sky.

Then an ear-splitting roar shattered the quiet. Followed by the rushing and pounding sound of massive wings.

"This is it..."

Katerina took a step forward into the light.

"...it's starting."

THE PRINCESS DIDN'T bother finding somewhere to change. She didn't bother with the notion of clothes at all. The second she looked up into the sky and saw a dragon, blind instinct took over and she went running out to the center of the unprotected field.

She heard Dylan shouting something behind her. Saw the gleam of the wizard's dark army as they stared at her from the shadows by the castle wall. But she didn't have time for any of them.

There was a single opponent on her mind. One whom only she had the power to destroy.

Time seemed to slow down as she sprinted fearlessly over the grass. Her fiery hair streaming out behind her. A cry of battle ringing from her lips as she lifted her arms to the sky. There was a strange rushing sound in her ears. An overwhelming heat rising from deep inside her body.

Then her arms vanished entirely. Replaced with a set of flaming wings.

She leapt high off the ground and was immediately airborne. Her body tearing apart and transforming on the fly. Replacing the princess with the dragon. The runaway teenager with the warrior—the light of her mother's fire blazing in her eyes.

It took her a moment to realize that the battle had started below. At the sight of her fiery transformation both sides had charged towards each other, screaming at the top of their lungs.

Men unleashed their weapons as they hurled themselves across the field. Vampires flew forward like wisps of smoky shadow, too fast for the human eye to see. There was a deafening wall of noise as the shifters tore themselves apart. Vanishing for an instant from the battlefield before hordes of snarling animals sprang up in their place.

It was impossible to keep track of any particular person. Even from such a high vantage point, there were simply too many in the fray.

Katerina thought she glimpsed a flash of white-blond hair—twirling a javelin before burying it in the chest of a royal guard. She thought she saw a flash of a chocolate-brown wolf, racing at the front of the Belarian army before disappearing suddenly in the sea of bloodshed below.

So high up in the night sky, it was impossible to tell anything for sure. And with the two sides of the battle as mixed as they were, it was impossible to rain down fire on one group without unintentionally harming the other.

Not that she had the time. Katerina was only airborne for a few seconds before a creature from her nightmares suddenly dove out of the sky.

Alwyn.

He was a small man in person. Tiny, really. Standing just up to her shoulder, with waves of billowing ivory hair. If she'd hoped that the dragon would match his stature, she was sadly mistaken.

Massive black wings stretched as far as the eye could see. A giant, writhing body flattened like an arrow as it made its way towards her. Razor-sharp teeth—each taller than a man—glistened like silver daggers in the light of the moon. And a pair of boiling red eyes locked onto hers.

She didn't have time to react. Didn't have time to do anything more than freeze, hovering mid-air, and watch as the enormous beast went barreling into her body.

It was pain beyond measure. Never had the princess felt anything like it before.

She let out a tortured cry as his teeth tore her body, as his claws ripped wildly at her ruby scales. As a dragon, the only fighting she'd ever done had been with her fire. She'd never even considered the other weapons at her disposal. The animalistic ones that did nothing to separate the princess from the beast.

He bit her again as the two tangled in the sky. A massive, writhing ball of necks, and wings, and tails. His teeth sank deep into her shoulder, and she shrieked in pain as a crimson rain of blood fell down from the sky.

She never saw the wolf that tore himself away from the fighting. The expression of absolute fear as he stared motionless at the sky. She was too busy trying to keep herself alive to see the way an armor-clad fae dove out of nowhere to save him, shouting words too far away to hear while a pair of royal archers fell dead at his side.

You want to dance, old man? All right—we'll dance.

With a roar of defiance Katerina twisted her body around, discovering that her smaller size meant an increased agility. She wrenched herself free of the dragon's deadly grasp and sank her own teeth into the back of his neck, shaking her head back and forth with fury.

He let out a strange, coughing cry. But before she could get a better grip he struck her with one of his powerful wings, sending her spinning flightless through the sky.

The world flickered on and off as she careened towards the earth, fighting for consciousness and completely oblivious to the people fighting just below. There was a chorus of screams from both sides when they looked up and saw the crimson dragon, falling like a comet out of the clouds. A second before Katerina hit the earth her senses returned to her and she spread open her giant wings, sweeping back to the sky on an upward current of air.

Alwyn was waiting for her, but this time she wasn't going to let him get too close. Even as he prepared for another catastrophic dive, she reared back and let loose a wave of fire, aiming it straight for his withered heart.

The wizard screamed and roared as it circled around him, scorching the air and dripping like lava down his charcoal scales. He tossed his head wildly, like he could somehow shake it loose, but before he could recover himself the princess hit him again. Even harder this time. Right in the face.

He screamed again. A sound so feral and frightening, that on the ground below the battle came to an actual pause as people gaped up at the sky. A barbed tail lashed out at the princess as he propelled himself higher into the sky, putting some distance between them before he tried to summon the fire for himself.

Tried... but failed.

Katerina's eyes flashed with a wicked grin. *Didn't learn that one yet, did you, old man?*

Neither dragon was able to speak, but she could have sworn the wizard guessed exactly what was going through her mind.

That's what happens when you take things that don't belong to you.

It was at that moment that his wings stopped beating. Hers froze in automatic reply. For a split second both dragons, the wizard and the princess, simply stared at each other. Then Alwyn spread his wings like the sails of a ghostly ship and dove straight out of the sky.

Katerina stared after him in shock, her pupils dilating to their fullest extent.

What the heck is he doing? Those are his people down there, too It's almost like...

The princess' heart froze in her chest.

...like he has another target.

Her mouth fell open as she streaked to the ground in what felt like slow motion, gasping little bursts of fire as she tried to pick up speed. He was already so far ahead of her, it was almost hopeless—but still, she had to try. Harder and harder she flapped her wings until her body was nothing more than a crimson blur. But then, just as fast as she'd been flying, she suddenly stopped.

She was too late.

The dragon was already holding Dylan in a claw.

Chapter 13

THE PRINCESS HAD TROUBLE remembering what happened after that. There was a sound of distant screaming, but she couldn't make it out over the ringing in her ears. There was the sense that something was burning, but she didn't know what it was until she realized tears of liquid flame were dripping down her face. Then, one sound in particular cut through the din.

It was a broken gasp. Hardly louder than a whisper. But it seemed to echo in the night.

Katerina's eyes shot down to see Dylan struggling weakly in the dragon's claw. At one point or another he had shifted back and was attempting to fight Alwyn off as a man. It was a brave but useless struggle. Already, the edges of his face were beginning to pale as torrents of blood spilled down the front of his shirt, pooling around the dragon's claw embedded somewhere in his chest.

There were other sounds now, too. Sounds of people scrambling down below. People yelling for each other, then detaching from the battle as they raced into the castle. Just a small, dedicated group, but Katerina didn't have to look to know exactly who they were.

She kept her eyes on Dylan. Streaking towards him as he was carried over the battle field and up into the sky. Closing in like a streak of lightning as Alwyn landed gently upon the roof of the castle and raised his claw. His eyes locked on the princess, and the silent message was clear.

He could no longer sustain this magic. As such, neither one of them would be allowed to use it any longer. If she didn't shift back into a human, he would kill the man she loved.

She didn't think. At this point, it wasn't even a question in her mind.

Even before she reached the stone roof of the castle, she began to shift. Dropping down the remaining twenty or so feet as a person, she rolled painfully to the side. Unable to hold out even a second longer, the shadowy dragon disappeared. Dylan fell with an excruciating gasp onto the cold stone as the door to the roof burst open and the rest of the group raced to his side.

"Where's Katerina?" he asked in a daze, lifting a hand to his head as he tried desperately to see over the others. "Where is she, I don't—"

"At last, dear one, it's just you and me."

The entire roof froze as the wizard walked slowly to the parapet. A fresh robe draped over his body and a silver knife glittering in his hand. It was the same weapon he'd shown them down in the dungeon. The one enchanted to pierce the princess' heart.

The wizard's voice was soft but steady as he lifted the deadly blade.

"I think the time for talking has passed, don't you?"

Dylan let out a silent scream as the knife flew through the air, burying itself in the heart of the woman he loved. Her auburn hair flew forward as she was lifted off her feet. Falling in what felt like slow motion upon the moonlit stone.

Her eyes fluttered shut as her lungs stopped breathing. A pool of blood was already seeping into the stones around her, and her body had gone terrifyingly still.

In just a matter of seconds, the girl he'd pledged his life to was utterly destroyed.

...then Katerina ran out from behind the stone wall.

She stared at the scene in front of her in utter confusion, one hand still raised to the back of her bleeding head where her fall to the roof had left her momentarily unconscious. She didn't understand the look of astonishment on Alwyn's face. The look of sheer horror on the others. She didn't understand why Dylan was staring at her like she was a ghost.

Then there was a shimmer of air, and she saw Tanya lying on the stone.

"NO!"

Cassiel shoved Dylan aside. Forgetting the wizard. Forgetting the battle. Forgetting absolutely everything except the tiny girl lying in a pool of blood. He raced across the roof and fell to his knees beside her. Pulling her head into his lap. Circling his arms around her lifeless body. Handling her with heartbreaking care, though it was clear she was beyond such things.

It was one of the first times Katerina could remember seeing him cry.

Little streams of crystal tears slid down his face as he cradled her against his chest. Leaning down so his forehead touched her own. Listening to the slow fade of her heartbeat, until eventually, and with a chilling finality, it came to a stop.

Katerina clamped her hands over her mouth. Dylan pulled in a faltering breath, then bowed her head to his chest. Serafina and Kailas were holding onto each other and Aidan looked like he was trapped in a horrible dream, gazing at the shifter's body with wide, unblinking eyes.

Why couldn't it have been me? Katerina's legs gave out where she stood as she gazed in horror across the length of the roof. *Why couldn't it just have been me?*

As if the skies themselves had heard her silent question, the clouds came together and started to rain. On the soggy field beneath them, the battle raged on. But the rooftop of the castle had never been so still. Every person there, even Alwyn, had frozen in shock. Unable to believe their own eyes. Unable to comprehend what they had just seen.

But then something strange began to happen.

Even stranger than all the rarities Kat had already seen.

Chapter 14

THE HAND CASSIEL WAS resting over Tanya's broken heart began to glow. A soft white light that started small, then spread to light up the air around them. Serafina let out a quiet gasp, taking a compulsive step forward, but Kailas held her back. Dylan's face blanched with the same speechless shock but he, too, stayed where he was. Silently watching. Rooted in place.

Cassiel was speaking now. Whispering words in a language Katerina didn't understand. His lips softly brushing his beloved's ear. As the rain came down around them, that soft glow of light brightened into a sudden halo. As if the heartbroken fae had called down his own personal star.

It hovered around him for a moment, shining like a beacon in his bright eyes, before slowly travelling from one to the other. Leaving the fae and entering the girl lying in his arms.

There was a sharp gasp, followed by an involuntary cough.

Then Tanya Oberon opened her eyes.

A gasp went up from the rooftop as that paralyzing sadness set everyone free. The others went rushing towards her, overwhelmed with shock and relief as Cassiel stroked her hair with a soft smile, his eyes twinkling down into hers.

Tanya blinked up at him. Staring like they were the only two people in the world.

"Am I dead?"

He kissed her softly on the lips, completely unconcerned with who might be watching. "Silly girl... you have to know I would never let that happen."

The rest of the gang gathered around them in a sort of protective circle. Half wanting to jump up and down in joy. Half hyper-aware that Alwyn was still with them on the roof.

Only one person didn't join in the celebration. She went to the wizard instead.

"Don't tell me that was the final trick up your sleeve," she said softly, glancing back to where the enchanted dagger crumbled to ash upon the stone. "I'll be so disappointed."

The wizard probably should have been scared. He should have been terrified. On the field below the castle, his army was close to surrender. He'd surpassed his capacity to channel his stolen magic, and the one thing that might have killed the princess had just crumbled into ash.

Yes, he should have been scared. But instead, he was a strange sort of calm.

"It wasn't supposed to be like this, you know." He folded his hands in front of him, staring at Katerina the way he used to when they'd take walks through the garden. Back when she was still a child. "None of this was supposed to happen."

It could have been a confession or an apology. Or simply just a statement of fact. Katerina wasn't sure. But the time for such things had passed.

"Someone once told me, we don't get to choose our stars," she replied. "This is what you made it, Alwyn. There's nothing you can say to change that now."

He nodded slowly, then abruptly lifted his hands. A flash of blue light shot out of them. The same kind of light he'd tried to use to kill her before. Only this time, it was somehow deflected.

"How..." he trailed off in shock. "How is that possible?"

Katerina gazed at him steadily. She didn't need to turn around to see what had happened. To see the way the light had been met with a force more powerful than its own. By her mother's fiery pendant, hanging safe and secure around Aidan's neck.

"This is for my brother and my mother..." she said slowly, lifting her own hands. A deadly fire started swirling in her eyes, dancing its way down her arms. "This is for me."

It wasn't flashy or dramatic. It was a single burst. A single devastating flame that buried itself in the wizard's chest before shooting out the other side. He stood there for a moment, staring down at the smoking hole. When he lifted his eyes, Katerina could have sworn he looked almost proud.

Then he fell to the ground.

Dead.

Katerina pulled in a silent breath as the raging fire cooled in her eyes. Fading to soft embers before vanishing entirely, leaving behind a sparkling grey. The rain poured down on her, soaking through her hair, cleansing the soot from her skin, washing the pools of blood off the stone.

After just a few seconds, it looked as though the entire thing had never happened.

A pair of warm arms circled around her waist and she leaned back into them. Closing her eyes in exhaustion. Feeling the beat of his heart against her skin.

"Are you all right?"

Dylan's voice whispered in her ear, and she shook her head with a quiet sigh.

"No... but I will be. We all will be."

It may have been a long time coming, it may have come at a heavy price. But it was over now. After all this time fighting, Katerina Damaris would take her rightful place on the throne.

For better or worse, it was done.

Epilogue

KATERINA STOOD ON THE stone balcony, looking out over the castle grounds. The grass was drenched in moonlight and her eyes shone silver with the celestial glow.

It wasn't long ago that this entire place looked very different. Littered with bodies. Drenched with pockets of blood. It had taken the survivors of the great battle two days just to work their way through the wreckage. It had taken twice as long to clean everything up.

Sometimes, when she wasn't careful, Katerina could still see the warriors. Still see the frantic clash of metal and hear the tortured screams. Sometimes, when she wasn't careful, she found herself getting out of bed in the middle of the night and walking silently over the grass.

Wanting very much to remember. Wanting very much to forget.

"You know it's creepy when you just freeze like that."

The princess turned around with a smile, staring at the beautiful man lounging in her bed. It was hard sometimes to come to terms with the fact that things were good now. That she could let herself be happy. That she could let herself relax.

Fortunately, her boyfriend was always quick to help her remember.

"At any rate, you're breaking your own rule," he chided sternly. "Remember what the two of us decided about clothes..."

She giggled aloud and slipped out of her bathrobe, climbing onto the mattress to join him in bed. Over the course of the last few weeks, Dylan had decided to stay in the High Kingdom under the guise of 'helping set up the new world order.' In reality, the two of them were having a delightful time discovering how far they could push things without actually going over the edge.

"Much better." He winked, lifting up the covers so she could slip inside. "You know I don't like to have to enforce these things, but I certainly will."

She rolled onto his chest, planting a grinning kiss right on his lips. "I think you like it a little bit."

He tried to smile back but winced instead in pain. "Babe, remember way back when I was pierced through the chest by a dragon...?"

"Oh—crap!" Katerina rolled quickly off his body, grimacing apologetically as he hitched himself stiffly up against the headboard. "I'm sorry! I totally forgot!"

He grinned mischievously, far more delighted by her horror than he was bothered by the pain. "Well, it wasn't *that* big a deal. Not considering everything else that happened that night."

The two of them fell silent for a moment. They didn't talk about the night in question very often, but it was getting easier and easier to do.

"Why did you give the pendant to Aidan anyway?" he asked suddenly. "I never asked."

Katerina nestled against him with a shrug. "He's one of the few of us who wouldn't shift and break it in the process. I figured he also had the best chance of surviving the battle itself."

Dylan glanced down sharply, his fingers wrapped around her bare waist. "What the heck is that supposed to mean? You think he had the best chance of surviving the battle?"

"You know..." Katerina bit down on her lip, trying to hide her grin, "because he's the best fighter and all."

There was a shifting of blankets as Dylan rolled onto his side, staring down at her with a dangerous kind of smile. "Is that right? The best fighter, huh?"

It was all she could do to keep from laughing. "Oh—by far. There's not really any competition."

He nodded slowly. "Is that right?"

Their eyes locked. There was a beat of silence. Then he was tickling her.

"*Wait!*" she squealed. "*Stop!*"

It was hopeless. Some slights were unforgivable.

Peals of breathless laughter echoed off the walls as he rolled on top of her, pinning her down with his legs as his fingers continued their merciless crusade. They wrestled and tangled together, and it wasn't long before he was laughing as well—both of them gasping for breath.

As was their habit, laughing soon turned to kissing, which soon turned to groping, which would soon turn to something else if Dylan hadn't pulled back with a sudden yelp.

"Damnit to he—!"

Katerina sat bolt upright in the bed, staring at him in concern. "What is it?"

He rubbed at his chest, giving her a rueful grin. "It's your bloody necklace. Why does it keep burning me like that?"

Katerina brought a hand to her neck with a smug grin. "It's magically bound to protect me, you know. Keep that in mind the next time you get the urge to—OUCH!"

She jerked her hand back, feeling oddly betrayed.

"It burned me, too!"

With delicate fingers she slipped it from around her neck, staring down with a touch of concern.

The fiery stone, which always burned brighter when she was with Dylan, seemed to have reached a new level entirely. One that sizzled at the edges of its gold frame and threatened to tear apart all together. On top of that it had never—not once—burned Katerina herself.

"Karma," Dylan muttered but he rested his chin on her shoulder, staring down as well.

She was about to put it on the nightstand, planning to consult with Petra about it in the morning, when a sudden tug almost jerked it out of her hands.

"Okay. What the heck is going on?"

She leapt quickly to her feet, slipping on her bathrobe, as the stone jumped and danced in her fingers. Every few seconds it would tug again on her arms, leading her to the door.

"Babe, get up!" she commanded, her eyes lighting up with wonder as she followed its enchanted lead. "I think it wants us to go somewhere."

"Are you sure it doesn't want you to get naked again in bed?"

She flashed him a look, and he pushed to his feet with a sigh. A minute later they were both dressed and heading out the door, following the amulet's fiery lead.

It was the middle of the night and the rest of the castle was still sleeping, but when they ran into the rest of their friends in the hallway Katerina shouldn't have been surprised. Ever since the five kingdoms had united in battle, the group of friends had been inextricably tied. Unnaturally bonded by the light of the amulet. Even more so than they'd been before.

"What is going on?" Tanya demanded. She was wearing a fluffy pink nightgown and her mohawk was curled up into little knots. "Cass and I were just... *minding our own business*, when all of a sudden we found ourselves getting out of bed. Met up with the rest of these losers in the hall."

"Minding your own business?" Aidan repeated with a quiet laugh.

"I mean we were having s—"

"Yeah, we got that." Serafina rolled her eyes and pushed to the front of the group. Hearing about her brother's personal intimacy wasn't her favorite way to pass the time, especially probably not when she and Kailas had been busy doing the same thing. "What's going on, Kat? Is it the amulet?"

"Yeah." The princess' eyes glowed as it burned bright in her hands. "It pulled Dylan and me out of bed, too. I think we're supposed to follow it."

There was a beat of silence.

"...or we could go back to bed," Cassiel suggested quietly.

Dylan threw up his hands. "That's what I said."

But adventure was calling, and the girls were up for a mystery.

After just a minute, and several muttered profanities later, the gang was heading down the stairs to the eastern wing of the castle. A place that was rarely used and even more rarely visited since suffering the most damage in the attack. They walked up one corridor and down another, the flaming stone burning like a beacon in Katerina's hand.

After a while, the whole thing was starting to look like a slumber party scavenger hunt gone wrong, and the princess was about to suggest that they call it a night, when it came to a sudden stop—right at an abandoned hall.

The gang froze in their tracks, then lifted their heads in unison to stare up at a painting mounted on the wall. A lovely portrait of Adelaide Grey. Faded through time, but still sparkling.

There was a hitch in Katerina's breathing and she took an automatic step back, feeling a terrible sense of déjà vu. "Please tell me it's not another tunnel..."

"It's not," Dylan had already swung the painting aside, revealing a tiny alcove hidden in the stone just behind. "It's a chest."

With careful hands, he pulled out the tiny box. Looking it over for a moment before handing it off to Katerina. She slipped the amulet, which had suddenly cooled, back over her neck before lifting its lid with a curious frown.

There was a single paper inside. A looping hand scrolled across old parchment.

Five kingdoms to stand through the flood
United by marriage, united by blood
Protected through grace, as only one can
To take up the crown, either woman or man

"What is it?" Tanya asked, trying to read over the princess' shoulder.

"I don't believe it..." Katerina held out the parchment, blinking in a sort of daze as she recognized a line of the writing. "I think it's the prophecy."

"What?" Tanya snatched it out of her hands. "Let me see."

She read it aloud to the group, paused, then circled suddenly back to a single line.

"Wait a second... united by marriage, united by blood? What is that supposed to mean?"

There was a faint *clinking* sound and the group whirled around to look at Dylan. He'd taken the chest back from Katerina and emptied the rest of the contents into his palm. A strange look came over his face before he held up his hand. He swallowed hard, uncurling his fingers so the others could see what he had seen.

A cluster of diamond rings, twinkling in his hand.

"I think it means somebody's getting married..."

THE END

... Or is it?

PROPHECY Blurb:

THE FIVE KINGDOMS MAY have been saved, but the battle is far from won.

Katerina Damaris finally takes her place on the throne, only to realize that the crown isn't what she thought it would be. Friends become kingdoms. Lovers become a liability. Secret promises are broken to protect the greater good.

Caught in the middle of political circus, Katerina must choose between ruling her kingdom or following her heart. Alliances are strained, borders are tested, and whispers of an old enemy resurrected hang like a shadow over the realm.

Can Katerina keep the peace? Will the five kingdoms ever be truly reunited?

Most importantly, can she and the others figure out the prophecy in time?

Note from Author, W.J. May

DEAR READER;

If this is not the first series you've read by me, you'll know how much I hate to say good-bye to my characters ? I'm a sucker for good relationships, friendships formed, family and fantasy.

In other words; Do you want more?

Let me know! I love to hear from my readers anytime!

Email: wanitamay@aol.com

Facebook: https://www.facebook.com/pages/Author-WJ-May-FAN-PAGE/141170442608149

UPDATE: More is here (and coming!)

The Queen's Alpha Series is now a 12-book series in the making!! Check out Prophecy – book 7 in the series!!

W.J. May

The Queen's Alpha Series

Eternal
Everlasting
Unceasing
Evermore
Forever
Boundless
Prophecy
Protected
Foretelling
Revelation
Betrayal

Resolved

Find W.J. May

Website:
http://www.wanitamay.yolasite.com
Facebook:
https://www.facebook.com/pages/Author-WJ-May-FAN-
PAGE/141170442608149
Newsletter:
SIGN UP FOR W.J. May's Newsletter to find out about new releases, updates, cover reveals and even freebies!
http://eepurl.com/97aYf

More books by W.J. May

The Chronicles of Kerrigan

BOOK I - *Rae of Hope* is FREE!
  Book Trailer:
  http://www.youtube.com/watch?v=gILAwXxx8MU
  Book II - *Dark Nebula*
  Book Trailer:
  http://www.youtube.com/watch?v=Ca24STi_bFM
  Book III - *House of Cards*
  Book IV - *Royal Tea*
  Book V - *Under Fire*
  Book VI - *End in Sight*
  Book VII – *Hidden Darkness*
  Book VIII – *Twisted Together*
  Book IX – *Mark of Fate*
  Book X – *Strength & Power*
  Book XI – *Last One Standing*
  BOOK XII – *Rae of Light*

PREQUEL –
Christmas Before the Magic
Question the Darkness
Into the Darkness
Fight the Darkness
Alone the Darkness
Lost the Darkness

SEQUEL –
> Matter of Time
> Time Piece
> Second Chance
> Glitch in Time
> Our Time
> Precious Time

Hidden Secrets Saga:
Download Seventh Mark part 1 For FREE
Book Trailer:
http://www.youtube.com/watch?v=Y-_yVYC1gvo

Like most teenagers, Rouge is trying to figure out who she is and what she wants to be. With little knowledge about her past, she has questions but has never tried to find the answers. Everything changes when she befriends a strangely intoxicating family. Siblings Grace and Michael, appear to have secrets which seem connected to Rouge. Her hunch is confirmed when a horrible incident occurs at an outdoor party. Rouge may be the only one who can find the answer.

An ancient journal, a Sioghra necklace and a special mark force life-altering decisions for a girl who grew up unprepared to fight for her life or others.

All secrets have a cost and Rouge's determination to find the truth can only lead to trouble...or something even more sinister.

RADIUM HALOS - THE SENSELESS SERIES
Book 1 is FREE

Everyone needs to be a hero at one point in their life.

The small town of Elliot Lake will never be the same again.

Caught in a sudden thunderstorm, Zoe, a high school senior from Elliot Lake, and five of her friends take shelter in an abandoned uranium mine. Over the next few days, Zoe's hearing sharpens drastically, beyond what any normal human being can detect. She tells her friends, only to learn that four others have an increased sense as well. Only Kieran, the new boy from Scotland, isn't affected.

Fashioning themselves into superheroes, the group tries to stop the strange occurrences happening in their little town. Muggings, break-ins, disappearances, and murder begin to hit too close to home. It leads the team to think someone knows about their secret - someone who wants them all dead.

An incredulous group of heroes. A traitor in the midst. Some dreams are written in blood.

Courage Runs Red
The Blood Red Series
Book 1 is FREE

WHAT IF COURAGE WAS your only option?

When Kallie lands a college interview with the city's new hot-shot police officer, she has no idea everything in her life is about to change. The detective is young, handsome and seems to have an unnatural ability to stop the increasing local crime rate. Detective Liam's particular interest in Kallie sends her heart and head stumbling over each other.

When a raging blood feud between vampires spills into her home, Kallie gets caught in the middle. Torn between love and family loyalty she must find the courage to fight what she fears the most and possibly risk everything, even if it means dying for those she loves.

Daughter of Darkness - Victoria
Only Death Could Stop Her Now
The Daughters of Darkness is a series of female heroines who may or may not know each other, but all have the same father, Vlad Montour.
Victoria is a Hunter Vampire

Don't miss out!

Visit the website below and you can sign up to receive emails whenever W.J. May publishes a new book. There's no charge and no obligation.

https://books2read.com/r/B-A-SSF-UMFS

Connecting independent readers to independent writers.

Did you love *Boundless*? Then you should read *Radium Halos* by W.J. May!

Everyone needs to be a hero at some point in their life. The little town of Elliot Lake will never be the same again after Zoe, a high school senior, and five friends take shelter in an abandoned uranium mine during a thunderstorm. Over the next days, Zoe's hearing increases drasticall... to supernatural levels. She tells her friends, only to learn that four others have an increased sense as well. Zoe is determined to use their abilities for good, while trying to keep her growing feeling for Kieran, the new boy from Scotland, under control. Fashioning themselves into superheros, the group tries to stop the strange occurences happening in their little town. Muggings, break-ins, and murder begin to hit too close to home. It leads the team to think that someone knows their secret - someone who wants them dead. An incredulous group of hereos. A traitor in their midst. Some dreams are written in blood.

Read more at https://www.facebook.com/USA-TODAY-Bestseller-WJ-May-Author-141170442608149/.

Also by W.J. May

Bit-Lit Series
Lost Vampire
Cost of Blood
Price of Death

Blood Red Series
Courage Runs Red
The Night Watch
Marked by Courage
Forever Night

Daughters of Darkness: Victoria's Journey
Victoria
Huntress
Coveted (A Vampire & Paranormal Romance)
Twisted
Daughter of Darkness - Victoria - Box Set

Hidden Secrets Saga
Seventh Mark - Part 1
Seventh Mark - Part 2
Marked By Destiny
Compelled
Fate's Intervention
Chosen Three
The Hidden Secrets Saga: The Complete Series

Kerrigan Chronicles
Stopping Time
A Passage of Time

Mending Magic Series
Lost Souls

Paranormal Huntress Series
Never Look Back
Coven Master
Alpha's Permission
Blood Bonding
Oracle of Nightmares
Shadows in the Night

Prophecy Series
Only the Beginning
White Winter
Secrets of Destiny

The Chronicles of Kerrigan
Rae of Hope
Dark Nebula
House of Cards
Royal Tea
Under Fire
End in Sight
Hidden Darkness
Twisted Together
Mark of Fate
Strength & Power
Last One Standing
Rae of Light
The Chronicles of Kerrigan Box Set Books # 1 - 6

The Chronicles of Kerrigan: Gabriel
Living in the Past
Present For Today
Staring at the Future

The Chronicles of Kerrigan Prequel
Christmas Before the Magic
Question the Darkness
Into the Darkness
Fight the Darkness
Alone in the Darkness
Lost in Darkness
The Chronicles of Kerrigan Prequel Series Books #1-3

The Chronicles of Kerrigan Sequel
A Matter of Time
Time Piece
Second Chance
Glitch in Time
Our Time
Precious Time

The Hidden Secrets Saga
Seventh Mark (part 1 & 2)

The Queen's Alpha Series
Eternal
Everlasting
Unceasing

Evermore
Forever
Boundless
Prophecy
Protected

The Senseless Series
Radium Halos
Radium Halos - Part 2
Nonsense

Standalone
Shadow of Doubt (Part 1 & 2)
Five Shades of Fantasy
Shadow of Doubt - Part 1
Shadow of Doubt - Part 2
Four and a Half Shades of Fantasy
Dream Fighter
What Creeps in the Night
Forest of the Forbidden
Arcane Forest: A Fantasy Anthology
The First Fantasy Box Set

Watch for more at https://www.facebook.com/USA-TODAY-Bestseller-WJ-May-Author-141170442608149/.

USA TODAY
BESTSELLING AUTHOR
W.J. MAY
bring fantasy to life...

About the Author

About W.J. MayWelcome to USA TODAY BESTSELLING author W.J. May's Page!

SIGN UP for W.J. May's Newsletter to find out about new releases, updates, cover reveals and even freebies!
http://eepurl.com/97aYf

http://www.facebook.com/pages/Author-WJ-May-FAN-PAGE/141170442608149?ref=hl

and

http://www.wanitamay.yolasite.com/

Please feel free to connect with me and share your comments. I love connecting with my readers.

W.J. May grew up in the fruit belt of Ontario. Crazy-happy childhood, she always has had a vivid imagination and loads of energy.

After her father passed away in 2008, from a six-year battle with cancer (which she still believes he won the fight against), she began to write again. A passion she'd loved for years, but realized life was too short to keep putting it off.

She is a writer of Young Adult, Fantasy Fiction and where ever else her little muses take her.

Read more at https://www.facebook.com/USA-TODAY-Bestseller-WJ-May-Author-141170442608149/.

Made in the USA
Columbia, SC
19 September 2021